Once Upon a Time in Hell Valley

Afshin Rad

Title: Once Upon a Time in Hell Valley

Author: Afshin Rad

Publisher: Supreme Art, USA

ISBN: 9781942912927

Preface

In late August 1987, a close friend and I went to a farm in southeastern Virginia to finish some paperwork about an inheritance.

This agricultural land was situated in a location that was not easily accessible, so not many people ever went there.

The only times of the year when outsiders were seen in the village were during harvest time and on special occasions.

Indeed, it had been a very long time since anything important had been cultivated there, and it had essentially gone abandoned and useless.

To tell the truth, I had completely forgotten that my ancestors had owned land and property in this area until our lawyer and family advisor told us about it with great excitement and asked me to go there as soon as possible.

When my wife heard this, she was so happy that she was walking on air. She thought that we had been given something important and valuable. She might have been right. If that wasn't the case, our family advisor wouldn't have asked me to quit my job and move to the other side of the country.

My father's family owned this land and the surrounding lands for a very long time. They were among the known landowners in this region at the time, and the public viewed them with a great deal of respect and acceptance.

In its heyday, this noble property encompassed close to one thousand acres, and it was home to hundreds of families who worked the land. This is something that was mentioned by other people, and it was also shown in the documents.

I'm not exaggerating when I say I didn't give my ancestry much thought. In some ways, I even felt humiliated and embarrassed!

However, it soon became apparent that there were more pieces of information that are concealed from view.

I was taking an inventory of equipment and making a list of assets when I happened to notice some half-rotten papers and manuscripts that were about my paternal ancestor's experiences during the Civil War.

The way these memories were told and written completely took my mind off of what I wanted to do and my main goal there, and it threw me into a different world.

After reading all the manuscripts and carefully looking at them, I was so taken with their strange and wonderful stories that I spent years organizing and re-editing them in the hopes of sharing this extraordinary and unique experience with others and opening their minds to new horizons.

I hope you enjoy the story and narrative that is now in front of you because it is a compilation of my ideas, fantasies, and personal convictions as a researcher and writer combined with actual historical events.

Table of Contents

Chapter One: Beginning

Between roughly 1760 and 1840 AD, the Industrial Revolution took place, laying the groundwork for profound and enormous shifts in a global society and its huge and stunning results and achievements can be felt today.

It was during the height of this era's progress and prosperity that political tensions and contradictions in the United States got more severe, and they eventually devolved into horrific and murderous confrontations.

This significant and influential historical event not only caused the growth and manifestation of the American society and changed its cultural and political structure, but it also formed the basis for the transformation of other human societies, and its beneficial results and effects, over the course of time, spread throughout the world.

Before discussing the primary storyline, I believe it is important to review and assess a sequence of events as well as significant and difficult political choices that stoked the flames that lay dormant beneath these ashes and propelled the American society of the time with great haste toward new frontiers and horizons.

On the 6th of November, 1860, following the presidential election, South Carolina voted to withdraw from the United States Congress and declare independence. Following this, the number of states that were under rebel or separatist control reached thirteen, and these states were referred to as the "slave states".

In these places, slavery was still official and legal, and there wasn't much hope that the situation or the way the law enforcers and politicians thought about it would change, unless something unexpected happened that made them have to change their ways.

During this war, the northern states, led by Abraham Lincoln, lined up against a large group of feudal lords and big landowners in the south, all of whom were led by Jefferson Davis.

Unquestionably, the abolition of slavery and discriminatory legislation were viewed as the primary motive and engine of this conflict, but other objectives and demands were also concealed. At first, this war was a fight between the elites and the favored classes, who felt that their goals and beliefs were being threatened.

Northern elites desired economic development: open borders, free labor, high tariffs to safeguard manufacturers, and the establishment of a new banking system throughout the United States. Their objectives and ideals were obviously at odds with the aspirations and interests of the slave owners, who benefited financially from their ownership of slaves.

To discourage more fighting and rebellion, Lincoln issued the preliminary Emancipation Proclamation in **January** 1863. This development augured further conflict and bloodshed in the ongoing battle. It was viewed as a strategy and a battle plan that further weakened the enemy side and increased the pressure on them.

Putting that aside, there were other changes at the core of society that gradually made people more aware of their rights and human rights. These changes led to a fundamental shift, especially in places where the wind of freedom and progress was blowing more strongly in the spaces and minds of its people.

The leaders of this broadening movement were, predictably enough, academics and civil rights advocates. They were willing to endure any difficulties in order to achieve their goals and realize their dreams.

One journalist claims that in the modern era, individuals are concerned with more than just meeting their basic physiological demands; they are also eager to obtain the rights and ideals necessary for the development and perfection of any civilization. But this is not sufficient on its own. They require strong and effective leadership to guide this collective resolve to fruition.

Without a shadow of a doubt, I would tell anybody who asked me that Abraham Lincoln is qualified and deserving of this position. He not only knew a lot about many things and had a lot of insight, but he also had a very attractive and charismatic personality that drew huge crowds of people to him.

Indeed, he was the type of leader who might help us achieve our deepest hopes and fondest ambitions.

He seriously pursued the establishment of basic principles to realize national independence and equality in this land. In reality, this perfection was desired by everyone, from intellectuals and civil rights activists to the lowest strata of society, which are colored people and slaves, because they were sick of the discrimination and injustices common in society and wanted fundamental changes and transformations.

But we also knew that it would take a lot of work from all the political parties and people who were fighting for freedom.

Saying that I was one of the first volunteers to join the northern coalition is not an exaggeration. My main objective was to move my country closer to peace and freedom in the future. That is to say, I had no desire for a celebrity or certain political or social causes.

Unsurprisingly, this decision shocked and offended several of my friends and acquaintances who lacked the patience to witness and embrace these societal shifts. Most of them came from southern aristocratic families that had lived the same way for generations, taking the crops of their subordinates as "booty" without giving it a second thought.

I don't intend to imply that every single person in the South approved of slavery and racial discrimination, but there were some taboos and limits that weren't easily crossed back then, especially for those of us like myself who can trace our ancestry back to this skewed social order.

At best, it caused our loved ones to turn their backs on us since they couldn't forgive such a heinous betrayal. This is how I felt when I first heard about this political and social fight.

I wasn't on the front lines for very long before the pervasive violence and cruelty there affected me, weakening my morals and beliefs and causing me to lose hope for a bright future. It was like I woke up from a deep sleep and found myself staring down at a naked and shocking truth that completely changed all my previous beliefs, attitudes, and points of view.

In this situation, a severe and fatal illness struck me, changing the course of my life.

I wasn't the only one hit by severe illness and weakness. Some diseases and their effects were unfortunately disseminated due to insufficient food supplies and terrible weather. They did not yet understand the connection between a healthy diet and a positive mental and physical state.

As a result, they gave this problem little consideration.

In the first few months of the winter of 1862, my health got worse to the point where my coworkers and friends were very worried and started coming up with ideas for what to do.

I was so thin and weak that I couldn't stand for long periods of time or carry my weapons and ammunition. I couldn't even face the enemy.

Colonel Sebastian Moreau, my boss, and a close family friend, told me to finally ask for time off from my battalion and stay away from the front lines.

Some weeks went by like this, with me hiding out behind the front lines to recuperate and regain strength, but it did not affect my health much.

My friends and relatives did everything they could to help me get better, but I showed no signs of doing so. I was dwindling and melting before their eyes like a candle.

It turned out that my illness was too bad for me to get better so quickly. In fact, I was ready for my death to happen soon.

It was a situation that didn't make me feel scared or worried at the time.

The colonel was like a brother throughout this ordeal, dropping by frequently to see how I was doing and offering comforting words of encouragement.

When he visited, he always brought me a little something to brighten my day. Wine and cigars, for example, were a source of blessing and joy for the troops.

Finally, he had me get out of the army and start taking care of myself properly.

Not far from the place where we had set up our camp, there was a monastery that housed several war-wounded and incurable patients.

The colonel had already recommended me to the officials there because of his brief acquaintance with them.

This location was in the heart of a high mountain, and it was nearly impossible to navigate its twists and turns, especially at that time of year when heavy snow covered everything. Even healthy and strong people would struggle with this task, let alone a sick and suffering person like me, whose mental and physical strength is dwindling by the minute. It was deteriorating.

They had given me enough food and medicine to ensure that I would not have any problems. If I got lost and wandered for a week or two, I'd have water and food in my bag to keep me alive, especially on the condition that I find a safe and suitable place to live. Otherwise, I would have been caught in the middle of a snowstorm and would have had no choice but to embrace death.

Since the colonel was worried, he sent one of the experts in the area to go with me.

Up until about halfway through, that guy stayed by my side and looked out for me. But he slowly pulled away from me, retreating into the depths of the mountains.

Worse, he took water, medicine, and a substantial portion of my meal ration with him! He simply left me some tobacco and a few pieces of frozen beef.

I was surprised by what happened because he seemed like a good person I could trust. If things had been different, the colonel, who was my boss but also my friend and constant companion, would not have taken the risk of leaving me in his hands.

I believe he abandoned me in this state as a result of my frailty and illness.

He presumably assumed that I had a contagious illness and avoided me. Many soldiers have recently died in this manner. So it was clear that he was concerned about this.

But why did he bring my food and medicine? Didn't he realize what I was going through?

It was possible that he had done it accidently, or that he had planned it ahead of time.

Whatever the situation may be, this was a horrible, cowardly act that will always stick in my mind. I never anticipated being put in such a perilous and difficult circumstance. He abandoned me deep inside a mountain that I knew would soon become so icy that it would consume me, flesh and bone. Despite this, I pushed through my uncertainty and dread and made progress. I mean, there was no other option. At least I knew where I was going because I had a thorough map.

As I moved deeper into this untouched, frozen landscape, I thought about what had happened in my life to bring me to this last chapter.

I have to admit that I did not live up to my beliefs and goals as well as I had hoped, and I did not achieve all of my deepest wishes.

The truth is that few people ever get to experience the fulfillment of all their hopes and ambitions.

Unfortunately, I was not an exception to this norm. On the other hand, I felt accomplished.

At least I can say that I was among the ranks of those who sought freedom and fought for ideals worth dying for.

It was the source of my heart's strength and encouragement during that trying and exhausting situation. I simultaneously hoped to find a cure for this deadly illness and find the strength to be ready to go back to my unit. But I was well aware that it would not be easy to make this wish come true.

Assuming I made a full recovery that still wouldn't guarantee my wish would come true.

This opportunity would only present itself to me if both my troops and my northern allies were successful in achieving significant victories.

When that happened, I was allowed to bring my unique flavor to these struggles. Things likely would have been different if that hadn't happened.

To put it another way, my main goal was to stay healthy so I could see what happened next.

As I was lost in these mental processes, the horrible sound of the cannons boomed in the cold and empty space of the mountain, and red dust spread across the battlefield.

At that time, there was a terrible hell behind me that no sane person would want to enter. Only those whose very selves were permeated by patriotism and the desire to defend those principles, or who were thrust into it against their will, felt any real obligation to do so.

There were untold numbers of people on both sides of the front with similar situations, and only time would tell how these violent conflicts would ultimately play out.

Thank goodness I was spared participation in that horrific bloodbath. I don't mean that I lacked the courage to face down the nation's foes head-on. You may take my word for it; that is not the case. The only reason I avoided this viewpoint was because of my health and temperament.

Undeniably, I wouldn't be able to execute my job successfully and instead would become a burden to everyone around me. As a result, it would be preferable if I could keep my wounded and sick body as far away from the front lines as feasible.

When I had to face this sad and unavoidable truth, my troubled conscience felt a little better.

In this challenging situation, several cannonballs hit the mountain's heights one after the other, causing a massive and violent avalanche.

Using all my might, I made my way to a solitary rock on the mountainside and sought refuge there.

If I waited too long to make my move, I would be buried alive like a speck of dust in a remote nook of the mountain.

When I was satisfied the threat had passed, I waited there for close to half an hour. After that, I battled my way back through the deep snow to the main drag.

I was doing this even though I was so tired and worn out that I was slowly falling down.

My life would have been in danger if I hadn't reached the monastery as quickly as possible.

It would not take long for scavengers and wild creatures to arrive at my lifeless body, leaving only bones behind.

Surely, this rough mountain had taken the lives of many people in this way, turning them into a part of its wild and beautiful scenery.

I thought at the time that I was stuck in a cold, lonely place and needed to find a way out as soon as possible.

The temperature fell significantly as soon as I stepped down the mountainside. Then a storm and heavy wind began to blow, making it difficult for me to see a few steps ahead.

I was searching for clues that would lead me to the monastery while the biting wind whipped at my face and head.

A large pine tree bearing the cross was included on the map.

Once I located the tree, I sat for a while at its base to rest my weary legs and lungs.

Initially, I desired to start a fire to warm myself, but the wind was too strong for me to search for firewood. In addition, I am surrounded by neither dry grass nor branches. With this circumstance, I could not stay there for an extended period. If I stayed still and calm for much longer, I would get frostbite and fall into a deep sleep that would never end.

Even for a brief minute, I believed that the angel of death had passed before my eyes. I saw him in the guise of a white-clad, heartless entity with a face that held one's breath in its chest.

He was probably hiding in the shadows and waiting for me to give up on trying to stay alive.

Naturally, surrendering to death under such conditions did not appear to be so painful and frightening. The camp doctor had told me in no uncertain terms that my physical strength would deteriorate over time and that the sickness would eventually consume my entire body. What if I could just go into a deep, eternal winter slumber and end this slow, agonizing death?

This flashed through my mind for a fraction of a second. But I could not allow myself to be subjugated by the impulse to submit to such a fate.

Once I had rested for a while, I got back up and continued my journey with renewed resolve, as the shadow of death crept closer and closer behind me.

I was in a rush to get there, but the environment and views were so breathtaking that I had to slow down and take them all in.

If you're reading this, you might be thinking that the way this point was expressed was weird or irrational.

Please wait while I answer your question.

A few days ago, the colonel paid me a visit, and when he was here, he raved about how beautiful this location is, and ever since then, I've been counting down the minutes till I can see it for myself.

I have to concede that he wasn't making things up at all. Even during this time of the year, visitors are able to take in a sufficient amount of this location's breathtaking scenery and unspoiled activities to be awestruck.

The waterfall the colonel had spoken so highly of was my top priority. The boundary line between the northern mountain and its lower slopes and this waterfall's location, as he put it, was in the center of a deep valley.

On the map, this marker was the most obvious. I probably wouldn't be able to get where I was going if I didn't discover it. I would be in big trouble in this situation. Thankfully, this did not occur.

When I heard the sound of falling water in the distance, I knew I wasn't lost and that I was on the right track.

Even though I wasn't feeling well and was counting the seconds until I could get to a warm and soft place, my soul was so filled with love for nature that I ignored this vital issue and moved toward the waterfall.

It meant that my tired, helpless body had to deal with more pain and pressure, and that most of the energy I still had was wasted.

In short, I struggled up the mountain's relatively steep slope until I reached the valley's edge.

As I got closer to my destination, I saw a beautiful scene that instantly made me feel better and helped me forget how tired I had been.

The waterfall, which appeared to be a river floating in space, was direct across the valley from me, emptying its waters into the rushing river below. When so much water came quickly and strongly to the surface of the river, it made a cloudy, ethereal mass that looked like a dreamy bed.

As I looked at this beautiful scene, I thought about how different and opposite the people were who were killing and fighting each other at the same time. They were unaware of all the splendor and beauty that would make a normal person want to think more about himself.

If we humans were a part of this natural environment, why couldn't we learn from it how to get along with other life forms?

I was immersed in these thoughts and dreams when an awful cry and wail suddenly broke the spell.

They had previously informed me that a variety of wild and predatory species, including wolves, mountain lions, and large brown bears, spend this time of the year in their shelter. However, there was always a possibility that I might get unlucky and become a target of one of them. I had to leave that place as quickly as I could.

In such a situation, the guide had advised me to go against the wind to avoid letting predatory creatures smell me. This counsel was entirely appropriate and accurate. But doing so meant leaving the main path, which might be equally deadly.

Finally, I made the risky decision to carry on in the same way.

When a dim light in the distance arose, it encouraged and bolstered my heart even though I hadn't yet traveled very far.

I gave myself a good push and drove my legs, which were buried in the snow up to my knees, to move and battle more to reach there faster.

If I waited much longer, the victor's razor-sharp teeth and claws would catch me and be prepared to tear and shred me to bits.

The map made it quite evident that there was a shortcut close to the abbey. They only employed this method in unique and urgent circumstances.

The renowned monk and a few of his close followers were among those who knew about this shortcut.

I didn't ask the colonel about it, but it seemed like they got along well with him and were close because they wouldn't have told him such a crucial secret otherwise.

He claimed to have had a brief acquaintance with the locals, but this was false.

In any case, I was quite fortunate to discover this secret route in that circumstance.

If I were a devout and religious person, I would attribute this event to God's kindness and providence rather than my often unfavorable luck. Of course, getting there wasn't as simple as I thought it would be.

Due to the heavy snowfall, the branches of the three- to four-meter-tall shrubs on both sides of this small road had bowed to the ground, giving it a corridor-like look.

I had to stoop a little and pass under them with my head and waist slightly bowed, as if I were bowing to reach this hallowed sanctuary.

At the same time, I took great care not to touch the tree's trunk or leaves. Otherwise, a large amount of snow would fall on me, making me sicker and frostbite.

Regardless, it took me some time to traverse this road and enter the monastery outside.

The first thing I ran into was a big iron gate that looked like a giant in front of me and kept me out of the monastery.

It had the effect of a barrier that cruelly divided this area from the rest of the world! However, this was not the only thing that shocked me.

In the upper portion of the gate, extremely sharp and thorn-like bars were positioned so that no one could easily pass through them and enter the inner area. In addition, a very powerful shackle with a large red cross in the middle was affixed to the main entrance! Several torches were ignited all around, so creating a distinct and enigmatic ambiance within this space.

When war and other deadly conflicts are occurring, the monks' desire for solitude and seclusion is understandable. But I was unprepared for the unusual barriers and fences I encountered. It's clear the locals had a healthy respect for the unknown, yet were terrified of it.

I decided to take a closer look at that side of the fence before making my presence known to the people of the monastery. As a soldier, I learned to never look before leaping and to thoroughly inspect every situation. Who knows, maybe passing through that gate would have put me in a worse and more unexpected situation.

Behind the massive Iron Gate was a broad plaza that terminated at a massive, castle-like home.

Complete darkness and dread pervaded this structure. To be honest, I didn't think anything besides me resided there. It didn't look much like a church or a cathedral. At least that's how things looked at first.

To be honest, I felt a weird terror and anxiety wash over me at that same moment, the likes of which I'd felt only during the height of the war.

The voice of reason in my head kept telling me to leave this area as quickly as possible and not look back. There just wasn't enough time or resources under the circumstances to accomplish such a task.

My safety was in danger to the point that I couldn't stand up straight because I was tired, hungry, and had frostbite. On the other hand, the power of nature wouldn't let me.

Even if the devil appeared to welcome me, I would still enter his lair with enthusiasm.

I simply didn't care where I got to.

I just wanted to escape this uncomfortable situation by going inside as soon as possible.

I would have spent my final night there if that damn door hadn't been opened for me, passing away without leaving behind any lasting impression. In my opinion, this particular death did not align with the ideal circumstances for a soldier, especially for someone who held strong values of patriotism and love for freedom.

Concurrently, I noticed a lot of religious statues that were all facing the entrance. The way these statues looked and the expressions on their faces evoked various impressions in the mind of the viewer. The statues on the right side of the gate were angelic in appearance. It seems that they welcomed the newcomer. On the other hand, the statues on the left side of the gate portrayed the immense sorrow and suffering that sinful and feeble-minded individuals endure. In other words, they showed how people should be punished for doing things that destroy their souls.

Undoubtedly, they had a specific goal in mind when they placed these statues in that location. It's as if they wanted to warn visitors and newcomers that if they don't watch what they do and say, they will be put through a lot of pain and suffering!

I was still in awe of these monuments when I noticed something else.

Next to a pile of dirt and snow that had been stacked along the fence, I observed freshly dug graves.

When I honed my senses, I observed a significant number of tombstones that had erupted from the frozen earth. Next to them are other tombs and family tombs covered with bizarre and menacing symbols and figures.

Now I was certain that I had correctly interpreted the map and had not gone to the wrong location.

However, I regret having set foot there. If someone else had been in my place and seen these visions, he would have been scared and suspicious, and he would not have known where they started or where they were going.

Anyway, I had no choice but to enter this location and seek sanctuary in its unknown shadows. No matter how hard I pounded on the gate and made noise, no one on the other side responded. It appears that nobody ever lived there!

Probably because of the wind and storm, they were unable to hear my screams. The screaming resembled moaning and pleading.

In this manner, difficult and agonizing seconds passed until I lost my patience and tossed a very large stone at the mansion. At the same time, I cursed the locals with some foul and harsh words.

I don't know if it was my luck or not, but this stone hit the right spot, causing a lot of commotion and disturbing the residents of the monastery as they slept. During this moment, a dim light shone behind one of the building's windows.

A short time later, a man carrying a lantern came out of the monastery. He looked around carefully, then shouted in a loud, clear voice:

- Please be aware that we do not welcome strangers, particularly those with malicious intentions.

I reacted angrily, saying, "Why are you spewing rubbish, man?" Instead of saying that, move a little closer to the person, you are speaking to.

I was on the verge of succumbing to my weakness and incapacity and losing consciousness at the time. I added to my previous assertion, shaking my numb, frigid lips once more, "I came here for treatment." "I also have a strong recommendation letter."

Then, I said the name of the unit I was in and the name of the commander I worked for, hoping that they had already been informed of my arrival.

For a few seconds, that person looked at me from head to toe. Then, he went back to the mansion and shut the door behind him without answering me. It was like he had met both a thief and an evil person with bad intentions. This behavior made me so furious and upset that I yelled even louder than before:

The weather is terrible; why in the hell did you leave?

I also cursed him in a nasty and offensive manner.

I never used foul language or was snarky, and I always maintained proper social behavior, even in the face of those who disregarded morals. However, I did not place even the slightest weight on my moral standards and ideals at that time. The only thing I wanted was to escape that bone-chilling chill. That which I have described to you would happen to me if I remained in a state of inaction and passivity.

I stood there for a few minutes until another person came out of the ugly building and said the same thing.

I attacked him with additional hatred and rage.

I have no idea why they were so cautious. Possibly, something had occurred that caused them to be so terrified of outsiders.

In conclusion, despite the difficulty, I was able to convince that man that I am not a threat to him. However, it took him some time to move his large frame and approach me.

After a few steps, I knew he had physical difficulty.

He walked with a hunched posture, as if he was carrying something heavy on his shoulders. Furthermore, one of his legs was limping slightly.

He had a disease or a physical defect that I would find out about sooner or later if I stayed in the area for any length of time.

He was in his fifties, and his face was covered in acne and pimples when he first approached me.

He took out a bunch of keys and opened the gate for me with a little effort and struggle, without saying anything or asking any questions. It's as if he's breaking open the door to a thousand-year-old prison or crypt.

At the same time, he said, dryly and rudely, "Follow me."

When he turned his back on me, I saw why he was walking so strangely. The poor man had a big hump that weighed like a shell on his bent back. So there was no reason to be more curious in this matter.

In general, I shouldn't have been astonished to encounter such images, because I had entered a facility where the majority of its residents were sick people and nuns who had departed the world.

The colonel said that healthy young men had no right to be in this area unless they were there because of something that could not be helped for a short time.

The reason for this was not hidden from anyone because they may be scared that sexual attraction could undermine their faith and values! Such ludicrous limits were imposed especially for this reason.

In other words, only those on the verge of death or those so repulsive that they did not attract special notice would enter this mansion. People with disabilities were also included in the same category.

When I was walking behind that man, I couldn't help but think to myself, "What purpose does this kind of life serve? With the delusion that one day he will enter heaven and receive compensation for all of his sorrow and misery, a person torments himself day and night for no reason. I hoped someone would ask them what a ridiculous thing this is. To get to a fictitious paradise, you deprive yourself of all of life's blessings. Do the exact things there that you've avoided your entire life because you thought they were sources of immorality. Why not apply your thinking to what you do?"

I have no idea who is going to read these notes or when that is going to happen. You may be giving yourself the impression that I'm a faithless and impious person. If I'm being sincere, I couldn't care less about it. Telling the truth is the most important thing to me, above all other values. Even if it turns other people against me, they dislike me more.

It should go without saying that I did some research in the realm of religion and studied various religious texts when I was at one of the sacred sites. Because of this, I am somewhat acquainted with the vibe of these locations. Based on my experiences, I can confidently claim that the breadth of lust in these settings is more significant than everywhere else.

There is no complicated rationale behind this observation. People's mental and physical ailments worsen, and they have more bizarre and vivid sexual fantasies when they are coerced into choosing a brutal, soulless life or forced to disregard their natural wants and needs. This can also happen when people are persuaded into choosing such a life.

According to one of the thinkers, no force on earth can restrain or stop when lusty desire and urge are raging. It is precisely similar to a full and ferocious flood that traverses the most inhospitable terrain and advances in an uncontrolled manner until it loses its strength and dissipates. Occasionally, it results in irreparable, unfortunate, and unhappy outcomes.

I am not sure how well this example conveys what it is that I am trying to say. I am only aware of one thing: humans' salvation does not depend on their ability to control their instincts and ignore their physical requirements.

You will likely take offense at these comments if you are a person who practices religion and considers yourself to be a believer in that religion.

There is even the possibility of not continuing to read the rest of the story. Despite this, I have no plans to cease expressing my thoughts and opinions openly.

At that moment, I was acutely aware of the potent odor of repressed lusts and desires emanating from my environment. I could also feel the oppressive presence of death and the annihilation of the human spirit, which looked both holy and demagogic.

I went into the monastery with these ideas in mind, hoping that everything I thought I knew about this place and its people was wrong because it was based on what I already knew and had seen.

To begin, we entered a massive hall with a high ceiling fashioned like a cone. The hall was very tall.

My attention was first drawn to the area by the large and magnificent chandelier positioned precisely in the middle of the ceiling. It was the first thing that I noticed as I entered the space.

This chandelier was lit by many candles spread around it, serving as its illumination source. It was not in the least bit easy to change out these candles or to turn on and off the lights. This is probably why most of these candles were out, and the hall was only partly lit.

My attention was also drawn to a group of strange and scary statues and paintings on display simultaneously in different parts of the hall.

Most of these works refer to the torture and wandering of the souls of sinners in horrific purgatory, as well as the domination of demonic temptations over the fragile human soul. There is not much evidence of God's grace and forgiveness in their writings.

Even on the front heater and the outer edges of the fireplace, they carved a design that subtly draws attention to the issues that are currently taking place. In addition, one of the things that caught my attention was the scriptural passages written on the wall. They seemed to be tablets that had been there for years, and the area took on a distinctive and ethereal hue due to their presence.

Naturally, this is under the assumption that we think of these things as being a part of our spirituality.

While I was reading and analyzing one of these tablets, I heard the man's harsh voice again:

"Keep sitting until the conclusion of the prayer and communion ceremony." "Can you meet the big sister later?"

I was somewhat shocked to hear this nickname and inquired about it.

"Who is that person?"

Because of how I was saying the big sister's name, the man got furious and told me that if I didn't respectfully say her name, I would be held responsible and punished.

Then he pushed me to a wooden bench in the hall's corner and reprimanded me:

"Remain seated until I summon you."

I sank onto the seat with some apprehension and trembling as I waited like an obedient child for permission to meet the big sister. I had the impression that I was about to meet a significant and high-ranking individual.

Before this, there was no record that I chose to keep quiet in the face of insults and bullying words and did not attempt to answer.

You can blame my weakness and hunger, which seriously impacted my strength, for this apathetic and almost cowardly response. In that situation, the only thing that mattered was finding something to eat and a warm and comfortable bed.

I was conscious that I could not have high hopes for this location and the pious and dogmatic servants who worked there.

On the other hand, I was not anticipating being a witness to something so offensive and degrading. Because of my illness and bad health condition, I thought I would at least be treated better.

.

If I were to check myself into a soup kitchen or a lunatic asylum, I would receive better care.

Now that I have made an effort to complain and have dipped my pen into the heart of the matter to express the truth allow me to tell you very openly that the only reason I consented to accept this predicament was to flee the scene of the war and the terrible effects it had. To put it another way, my infirmity and physical ailment were nothing more than an excuse to escape that horrible and inhuman environment for the time being.

It didn't mean I gave up all my moral standards and principles and went in a different direction.

I needed only a small amount of rest and mental tranquility to prepare my fatigued body and soul for the crucial and dangerous days ahead. However, it appears that I did not step in the correct location.

Everyone is familiar with the living conditions in monasteries and convents.

We are dealing with extreme backwardness in these places even now, let alone in earlier times when prejudice and superstition were more overtly present in the community and in places of worship.

If I were to give an accurate description of this location, I would say that it did not have any vitality and did not promise anything for the future. I had the impression that I had entered a setting that was even more horrifying than the battlefields. While thinking about these things, I could hear coughing and wailing sounds coming from nearby.

These strange sounds emanated from the corridor on my right.

My curiosity prompted me to get up and look there. During this time, many frightening thoughts and imaginations flooded my mind.

Everything there was strange and scary, making anyone intelligent and observant feel sad and worried about his surroundings.

Let's move on.

Compared to the main hall, the corridor had a significantly lower illumination level, making it difficult to see what was on the other side. The only illumination source was a small number of candles placed in a recess in the wall's corner.

There was neither a window nor a door that led to the outside. It was as if they were trying to hide the demons and monsters.

As I went further, I found rooms that looked like cells. They were all on the left side of the corridor.

It appeared that patients and those in distress were kept in these chambers.

My suspicions about this matter were heightened when I noticed that some soiled sheets and articles of clothing had been piled on top of one another in a nook of the corridor. There was also a foul smell similar to the smell of corpses and dead people on the battlefield.

Initially, I believed that soiled sheets and clothing caused this foul and repulsive odor. When I honed my sense of smell, I understood that the odor emanated from those rooms.

I took a step closer, holding my nose with one hand, and peered through the crack in one of the doors.

In each of the three corners of the room or the crypt, there was a bed on which a very sick and suffering individual was writhing in agony.

The lighting was so dim that I could not see his face. I could not confirm whether he was male or female.

The only thing that was clear and not hidden was that he would die painfully soon.

This dreadful end may be in store for me as well. The only advantage I had over the other area residents was my relationship with an acquaintance with one of the high-ranking northern officers. They had a stellar reputation in that region. However, it was conceivable that the war's status could shift at any moment, and so on.

Even in this circumstance, they treated me poorly. Consider what would happen if I lost my leading supporter. In brief, I was in a difficult situation.

Since I first set foot in this location, a voice has been whispering in my ear:

You should leave this area immediately. If you do not repent, you will experience unimaginable pain and suffering.

I had heard this warning signal before, just as I was getting ready to join the front lines of the war.

My poor father exerted great effort to dissuade me from making this choice. He agreed to transfer all of his authority and responsibility to me.

I had been waiting for years before I could finally take advantage of this beautiful and alluring opportunity. In the end, however, I went with the path that was consistent with and honorable to the dictates of my conscience. If I didn't do that, I would feel like a terrible person for the rest of my life and have a guilty conscience whenever I did anything. I was unable to imagine any other course of action for my life.

Since I started this job, I've had to deal with a lot of problems and pain, but the worst was losing my physical and mental health. But I was happy and satisfied with my choice and proud of my service when I thought back on it.

Before his death last winter, my father wrote me a passionate letter in which he somehow apologized and consoled me.

He went even further and freed some of our slaves from hard work on the family's estates because he wanted to make me happy and satisfied.

Who could believe that I am the heir of one of the South's largest landowners? My father owned and controlled hundreds of slaves, who he treated like domestic animals. He managed to get rid of them whenever he thought they were no longer useful to him. I can't hide this painful fact.

Even though I haven't seen anything like that myself, I've heard from many different people that my father has done horrible and humiliating things to these poor people.

Only in the final days of his life did he understand the errors he had made.

The emancipation of the enslaved people was a significant step and a source of optimism, but it's a shame that he realized his mistakes too late.

Thank God that he did not depart this life in ignorance and hatred.

My father and I were the only ones in my family and circle of friends who had given up their old ideas and beliefs and started living a new way.

Each of us, of course, had our own reasons and motivations.

One of us fought for ideas and values that are important and necessary for the progress and excellence of any civilization. The other, who had given up his old prejudices and narrow-mindedness, fought mainly for the safety and survival of his family.

If these societal changes did not occur, he might continue to live in this manner for the remainder of his life. I do not mean that he pretended to transform and alter himself.

He deeply regretted his previous deeds and conduct. If I were truthful, I would acknowledge that he saw the need to revise and adjust social laws far before I did.

Because of his status and social standing, he was unable to reveal this secret and reveal his true position. If he did, he would enrage those who had stood by his side his entire life and supported him under any circumstances.

This work endangered his dignity, social standing, and family. Because of this, he rejected me and deprived me of my inheritance.

This continued until the warfare came close to our family's land, which made him and others sound the alarm.

At the time, there was a rumor that all major landowners and landlords involved in the slave trade had been brutally killed, and their properties had been taken as hostages.

It was only a rumor. But it made masters and enslavers scared and worried, so most ran away.

My father was one of the few people who stayed on the family estate. He wrongly thought he could control the situation and avoid the consequences.

He just sent my mother, my sisters, and a few other people who worked in the house to a different place.

I had left home a few months before this happened, so I didn't know where they were until I got a letter from my dad, which made me feel much better.

These wars and brutal conflicts undoubtedly cause several mental traumas that incapacitate both sides. Occasionally, it serves as the foundation for additional political and social distinctions and categories. On the other hand, the fact that liberty and democracy are not attainable through any other method cannot be hidden.

In other words, this is not a gift that can be given to people without causing pain, and getting it will require a lot of sacrifice and self-denial.

When you obtain it, you must tend to it as if it were a newborn kid so that it can go through the stages of growth and development and mature over time. It only takes a little bit of carelessness and tolerance in this way for the ugly and terrible monster of tyranny and autocracy to rise from the depths of corrupted minds and drag us back into tyranny and autocracy until the touch of freedom once again seems far away and impossible to reach.

We will move on from this issue and continue with the story, hoping you have the motivation and desire to follow this narrative and plot.

I was wondering when I suddenly heard a woman's voice from behind me:

"You must be Mr. Nicholas Mortimer."

When I turned my head, I noticed a tall, slender nun standing near the corridor's entrance and staring at me with a hostile face.

Under the dim candlelight, that woman's face had become odd and terrible. It seemed like a vampire had risen from her coffin and searched every area for prey and fresh blood.

She was covered from head to toe, as were all the nuns, except for her face, which lacked a hijab similar to a seed enclosed within a dense and multilayered sheath. Her actions and movements likewise lacked any trace of femininity or elegance.

This simplistic and dogmatic group believes they will avoid sin and maintain their holiness and purity. This method of thinking is ridiculous and dumb, and it has had no value and does not have.

Such religious and ethical understandings, in my opinion, are not only harmful to the individual and society, but also have unintended consequences. In fact, these perceptions deny people the opportunity for further growth and prosperity by erecting barriers between people and spreading superficiality and incorrect judgments throughout society.

The person in front of me was the purest example of this type of person. I would not say I liked having close relationships with those with whom I shared no common ground. But I followed the rules of politeness and talked to him in a kind and respectful way.

"Yes, sister, my name is exactly this. In addition, I also have a recommendation letter. Please permit me to give it to you."

She stated in a dry and impersonal manner,

"That letter of recommendation is unnecessary, sir." I've already talked about you with the colonel."

She then turned her back on me and walked to the opposite end of the hallway. Her behavior was obscene and offensive; it was as if she did not care about my presence or absence. Still, I had no choice but to deal with this situation, hoping to get out of there as soon as possible.

This opportunity would only be available if my illness were magically cured or if I were to die and thus be released from this new ailment.

While I was walking behind her, I asked her:

"I hope this doesn't pose an issue." I mean my stay here.

She said without looking at me:

"No. I only need to discuss some rules and regulations with you. I hope you are submissive and obedient. If not, we will encounter an issue."

"I am a soldier, sister. Therefore, I have no objection to the implementation of directives and regulations. Certainly, so long as it is accurate and sensible."

The big sister stated emphatically:

"Here, there are no ifs or buts. You must abide by the rules without challenging them. That's it."

I continued in a calmer tone:

"Sister, I am not a nasty person. Rest certain that I will not cause you any trouble!"

She murmured, "We shall see, young guy," under her breath.

Her tone and expression were menacing and suspicious. She was right to be worried.

All people who knew me well understood that I do not refrain from using aggressive and irrational language and fiercely defend my rights and human rights.

Because of my values and spirit, I regularly used to get into trouble with group leaders, high commanders, and superiors, as well as getting into trouble myself.

I cannot recall how many times I've been scolded for this issue. Believe me that I don't care to that either.

As mentioned earlier, the only thing I believe to be significant and valuable is taking a position against injustice and oppression while also telling the truth. If the circumstances had been different, I would never have participated in such a bloody and horrible battle and fight.

The big sister did not know me before. However, she realized I did not want to compromise with her.

In such a case, it was prudent not to annoy her further or to question her rules and ideas.

I was not a candidate for this treatment, whether by chance or design, even though I knew the outcome would be my loss.

She became quite enraged and attacked me when I questioned her about the patients housed there and criticized the manner in which they were kept and cared for as being inappropriate and inhumane. I felt as if I had done a serious sin that could not be forgiven.

It appears that no one could have entered that hall without her consent. This law was for everyone who lived in a monastery except those whose presence was required.

I attempted to flatter her, prevent her from escalating her rage, and finish the conversation. This approach was somewhat helpful and practical.

The big sister regained her composure and stated, "I will ignore this." Because you are a novice and have not yet become acquainted with the rules and regulations governing this site, I hope you will be more mindful of your behavior.

I continued in the same manner:

"Rest assured, Sister. Now, if you don't mind, may I ask one more question?"

What question?

"I want to know why there are no nurses and caregivers in the area. Due to their condition, these people should get ongoing attention. Is it not so?"

She answered:

"They are currently quarantined with a local doctor's prescription. According to the doctor, their disease may be contagious; therefore, we must quarantine them."

I continued:

"I understand, Sister. However, it is preferable to consider cleaning here. These sheets can at least be removed from the hall. This scenario is truly beneath the dignity of this location!"

Consider this last statement as flattery, which I have always despised and avoided expressing. In truth, I said this to mitigate the bitterness of my previous statements. But it did not work.

The big sister once again lost her mind and remarked in a manner reminiscent of the orders and prohibitions of stern and strict military commanders, saying, "Sir, we are well aware of our responsibilities. You are not required to teach us anything. Now follow me so I can show you around your room."

She then grumbled her way to the staircase on the opposite side of the hall. I followed her like a submissive slave.

Then she groaningly moved toward the steps on the opposite side of the corridor.

As I climbed the steps behind him, my eyes suddenly went black, and I felt slightly disoriented. Without leaning against the side wall, I would have likely lost my balance and plummeted to the ground.

This was because I was fragile and hungry, putting a double burden on my sick body.

The big sister had observed this. However, she exhibited no specific response. It was as if she had observed an ordinary occurrence.

It should come as no surprise that there was no reason to be shocked.

It is said that a person will get thick-skinned or impassive and become less compassionate over time if they are routinely confronted with people who are ill or nearing the end of their lives. This change and growth happen over time, especially during the war, when physical and mental wounds are the worst.

This rule did not exempt the big sister. However, her human and moral responsibility required her to pay greater attention to me.

After showing me my room, she summoned a servant to bring me food.

This was the least amount of consideration and courtesy she could show me.

Before departing, she spoke in a kinder, friendlier tone:

"The prayer ceremony is held extremely early in the morning. But since you just came, you can rest a little more."

I said politely and humbly,

"Thank you very much for your kindness." I am not a particularly religious person. If the prayer ceremony is not required, I prefer to stay in my room and rest all day.

Hearing this, the big sister became so enraged and upset that the color of her face changed dramatically, and many signs of anger and rage appeared on her face. It was most likely the first time anyone had taken such a strong stance against her faith and beliefs and challenged her.

However, she kept her calm and responded,

"Prayer is part of the treatment steps here." It has also been shown to be effective in calming the mind and spirits of patients.

I inquired with a smile on my face,

"So why doesn't it help those poor people?"

I was talking about the same still on the lower floor.

The big sister got mad at me for making snide comments and the disagreeable hints which made her blood boil.

She was just on the verge of losing control and whipping me with her words even harder.

Before this occurred, I stated calmly and expediently,

"I have no doubt you have excellent intentions." However, it would help if you did not force someone to act against their will. Ultimately, this work is not advantageous to any party and drives individuals apart.

As I had anticipated, the calming and conciliatory comments I made had minimal impact on her and did nothing to reduce the anger and inflammation she was experiencing. I thought I was pouring water on a solid, impenetrable rock, hoping that a hole would eventually form.

She gave me a look filled with disdain and cynicism and added,

It is common knowledge that you still do not comprehend where you have stepped.

I said, "Sister, I don't want to debate you on these matters; I respect your views and beliefs." But I'm not prepared to lose in the face of solid and irrational words."

This phrase infuriated the big sister even more since it cut straight to her heart and soul like a snake.

But despite her best efforts, she could not produce a firm and persuasive response to place in my hand while searching her mind's dark and empty recesses.

After a brief pause, she stated in a tone and manner that conveyed her inner anguish and unhappiness:

I asked the colonel to thoroughly explain everything to you. However, it appears that he made a mistake in this matter. He should have told you how this place works and how it is governed. I had no idea the colonel would send someone so stupid and skeptical here.

I continued with composure:

So, you allow only faithful individuals here? Therefore, a person who does not believe in these matters cannot receive your kindness and mercy. Did I hear you correctly?

The big sister gave me a very hostile and menacing look and said:

These phrases reek of skepticism and atheism. It appears that your spirit requires more polishing than your body.

I responded with a scornful tone:

If having faith means what you think it means, then you can count me among the unbelievers and atheists. In reality, this is my source of pride.

The big sister glanced at me in bewilderment for a few moments. Then, in a state of worry and perplexity, she exited the room and closed the door behind her so tightly that the upper latch broke loose!

I was still amazed when one of the servants walked into the room without knocking or asking permission.

He brought me a small amount of food, and he was a weak, skinny man. Anyone who saw him would feel sadness and sympathy for him due to his frailty and emaciation.

But what attracted my attention at first was not his overwhelming physical weakness.

The poor man was holding a tray of food with one hand, and with the other, he was gripping a crucifix dangling from his frail neck.

He was also murmuring something he couldn't understand, possibly a prayer to keep off evil spirits.

I gave him a heartfelt thank you and moved forward to grab the food tray, but to my astonishment, he drew back and walked the other way! He felt a hideous thing had appeared and was attempting to take control of his spirit.

I asked him why he was acting this strange and unexpected way, but he didn't answer.

He didn't say anything during his brief period of unconsciousness. She then made a prolonged, cautious turn to face me, studying me strangely from head to toe.

His bare and bony face showed symptoms of worry and uncertainty at that moment. It looked like he had gone to a place where demons and goblins lived.

He jerked and shook as he put the platter on the bed and waited in an odd position.

I asked him:

Why are you standing there? Are you hoping for a tip?

He answered in a shaky, broken voice.

No, sir, I'm waiting for you to finish a few bites of your food; I'm checking to see if the food satisfies you.

I had no reason to believe him. I could tell he was trying to hide something from me, but I was hungry and tired, so I didn't ask any more questions and just left him alone.

A few pieces of dry, nearly stale bread was accompanied by a few cloves of gritty garlic, a glass of milk, and some rotten cheese! It was nothing unusual that he wished to solicit my views!

Under normal conditions, I could not consume such cuisine.

However, I was so weak then that I ingested every piece of trash with my whole heart.

At least I did not go to bed hungry.

It was not clear that what this mixture would do to my stomach and intestines.

I must inform you of another peculiar aspect of this dish and its accompaniments.

In ancient times, people believed garlic had a unique and mystical power and employed it as a repellent against evil spirits.

They presumably placed the garlic close to my dish for this reason.

My unexpected arrival and the subsequent actions I took did not go over well with this superstitious and bigoted group. Because of what I did and how I came in, their twisted minds quickly filled with bad ideas and thoughts about me.

They likely believed a vampire had entered their supposedly safe and holy area.

I was willing to wager that they had blessed the milk and the bread to gauge my reaction.

To reassure him and the other superstitious individuals, I took a piece of dry bread and began chewing it as if I were eating a complete and delicious meal. In addition, I ate a whole clove of garlic to make him feel completely at ease!

You might not believe me. But when the man saw this scene, he exhaled a sigh of relief and left the room.

After he left, I threw my belongings into a corner and collapsed onto the bed like a corpse.

They had made a bed for me, but it was so uncomfortable and complex that it wasn't much different from the pavement and dirt of the streets!

It seemed like everything had been built there to make the pain worse and force the people there to be physically demanding.

At least I could be thankful that they gave me a bed sheet that was largely tidy and clean.

While lying down, I looked around at the gloomy and chilly surroundings.

It was in no way appropriate for anyone who was ill or in agony to live there. They hadn't even turned on the fireplace.

I admit that my arrival was somewhat sudden and unanticipated, but I was not prepared for the circumstances that arose. I have never been someone who is prejudiced or makes snap decisions. Even when things were at their worst, I made it a point to ignore pessimistic thoughts and focus instead on being optimistic.

This moral and character trait has greatly assisted me throughout my life and helped me become more patient and determined in the face of challenges. On the other hand, it did not seem very helpful or encouraging in this location!

After removing my drenched and filthy clothing, I smoked a cigarette and pondered my vague and unknown fate for a few moments.

Then I crawled naked under the duvet, convinced that I would soon fall asleep.

However, this did not happen! I have no idea what the rationale was. Was it the fact that I was in a strange and unfamiliar place that kept me from falling asleep, or was it the worry in my mind and the flood of strange and upsetting thoughts and dreams that kept me from finding comfort and peace?

I had trouble with the same thing when I got caught up in sexual thoughts and fantasies.

The big sister was at the peak of these erotic fantasies!

I imagined her approaching my bedroom in the middle of the night and quietly calling my name. I pretended to sleep to determine her intentions.

She cautiously tiptoed on my bed and gently pushed my coverlet to the side. Afterward, she looked at me with insatiable lust from head to toe. It is as if she is encountering the body of a man who is only partially clothed for the first time.

She repeatedly walked away from me while pleading with God to find a way to rid her body and soul of this evil longing, but nothing took place.

She was in a state of extreme bewilderment and had no idea what action to take, precisely like a person who is caught in a difficult situation and is unable to choose the best option.

Should she give up all her beliefs and values to satisfy her sexual need and desire, or should she hide in her celibacy and spiritual and physical austerity, refusing herself all the pleasures and gifts the world has to offer?

After some hesitating and fruitless struggle with needs that had been repressed for a lifetime and had finally erupted, she eventually removed her veil, pretended sanctity, and laid down next to me. Because she was nervous and excited simultaneously, her entire body was shaking slightly at that very moment.

This was her first sexual interaction or encounter. Thus, it was inevitable that she would locate such a state.

The harsh sound of her breathing, which was filled with insatiable passion, and the pleasant feeling emanating from her body's warmth had submerged my entire existence in the pleasure of wanting to sleep with her. I didn't give up, though, and I stayed in the same position until she put her warm lips on my poor, hurt skin.

I could no longer take it and emerged from my fabricated cocoon.

When I turned to her, she immediately moved backward and adopted embarrassed, shy demeanor. On the other hand, before she could take any action, I hugged her promptly while simultaneously kissing her from head to toe passionately. If I hadn't acted so quickly, it was possible that dread and uncertainty would have taken over her, and I wouldn't have had the chance to make love to her.

Because the big sister was so immersed in her pleasure and desire, it is impossible to describe her with words adequately. Imagine a person roaming for a long time in a desolate desert, searching for a mirage from here to there. Then, suddenly, she finds a crystal-clear spring that flows from the center of truth instead of illusions and false and empty ideas.

The big sister was essentially in this predicament.

She was learning about and interacting with a world she had previously shunned. Before I was discovered and the seed of doubt was sown in her heart, she didn't even dare to consider it.

It was like this, at least in my vivid fantasies and imagination.

As my insomnia persisted, my sensual fantasies grew increasingly vivid.

The big sister instructed me to curse at her and spit in her face! To say bad words or other rude things to her, for example, when most people wouldn't dare.

I declined to use dirty words and begged her not to ask me to use derogatory or obscene language. She persisted, though, and kept pleading with me to humiliate her.

There was nothing else she could do except throw herself at my feet and beg me to carry out this action.

Many people may look at these ideas and fantasies and consider them to be insane and sick. However, it has the potential to catch anyone in some way.

The big sister was so caught up in the sexual excitement and pleasure that she completely disregarded her convictions and lost all sense of decency as she acted unrestrainedly. This work brought her pleasure and a sense of sadistic fulfillment, making her feel more satisfied than ever before.

When I was ruminating on these ideas and visions, I suddenly recalled a lovely poem like this: "Her body and soul were like a blazing and endless desert that required continuous and heavy rain." "I had to flow through her like a raging river for all her dry and scarred cracks to heal and for her to become fertile like lush and wonderful meadows."

Someone like the big sister was portrayed in this poem written by one of my other good pals.

Both of them were held prisoner by their biases, which made it hard for them to connect and enjoy their lives as much as they should have.

I resolved that I would not be one who caved in the face of unavoidable circumstances. I had no qualms about breaking the laws and taboos of society to achieve the goals and rights that I desired, even if it meant that doing so was essential to achieve those goals and rights.

But at this moment, there was nothing else I could do but completely submerge myself in the enchanting realm of dreams.

The big sister repeated her request, "Please cuss at me and humiliate me in any way you see fit."

I complied with her request without any remorse or hesitation. The older sister felt great satisfaction and pleasure in this making love, and thereafter, she was lost in an imagined state of tranquility. She behaved as though she had experienced famine before entering a place of blessings and joy.

Chapter Two: Snowman

I awoke before daylight had fully arrived. My sleep and comfort had been disturbed by the nuns' concelebrating and praying, but I was not too concerned about it.

It was clear that I managed to avoid going to this depressing and dull event. That allowed me to get back to bed and catch up on some sleep. Actually, this was my first triumph against the big sister.

Skip this subject. You would undoubtedly concur with me that sleeping in the mornings is quite lovely and alluring, especially when you are pressed for time to get out of bed.

Since I was a young boy, I habitually have got up extremely early in the morning in order to assist my father and the other people who worked on the farm.

Having this characteristic and demonstrating it in my actions made it a lot easier for me to get through the challenging circumstances I went through while serving during the war. Having said that, living in this place was in no way comparable to the period that I spent serving in the military, and as a consequence, I developed into a new person.

At that time, the only thing that was important to me was to be left alone so that I could sleep and take a nap until noon without anyone disturbing me.

While I was basking in the glow of this euphoric sensation, I was surprised to see that someone I didn't know was in my room.

He was staring at me while he sat on the chair that was next to the fireplace.

When I saw this scene, I couldn't close my eyes to go to sleep, and I felt a little scared.

Before I could respond or say anything, that guy remarked in a calm, kind voice:

"You don't need to be terrified, young man. I'm one of your friends."

He finally got up after struggling for a while and walked over to me.

He was an old man, and because of his long, neat mustache and beard, he reminded me of my grandpa, who lived with us for the last few years of his life.

In general, at first glance, he seemed mature and reasonable.

I asked him very politely and respectfully to introduce himself and tell me why he was there at such an odd and inopportune moment.

In the same friendly way, he went on:

"I'm sorry for coming in without your permission. Sincerely, I came to welcome you on behalf of the rest of my friends and myself."

"You are extremely kind, but why are you here so early?"

"Curiosity drove me; I wanted to find out who was causing all the uproar last night. I've been told that you badly ruffled the big sister's feather."

"How did you find out?"

"I learned about it from one of the nuns. It appears that you have severely infuriated her."

"Hell with her. Who cares?"

"You will learn the truth sooner or later. Leave it. I intended to return when I noticed you were asleep, but you removed the sheet."

"At that moment, you had no underwear on, and I was afraid one of the big sisters would enter the room unexpectedly and see you like that. This is why I covered you with a sheet and waited for you to awaken."

"I wonder what would happen if one of the nuns saw you with that erected penis."

Hearing this made me feel a little embarrassed and humiliated, and I apologized to him for seeing such a thing.

The old man said with a smile on his face:

"Oh, young man! There is nothing to be embarrassed about. When I was your age, I used to be like this a lot. I believe the reason for this is the uncomfortable thoughts that run through our minds just before falling asleep, especially in a situation where the mind is more preoccupied with these issues. I'm glad to meet you in any case."

"Me too. If you don't mind, I'd like to put on my clothes right now. I'm a little uneasy about this circumstance."

Immediately after that, the old man turned his back on me and waited for me to put on my clothing.

While I was putting on my clothes, I asked him:

It seems like you have been living here for a long time. Haven't you?

"It isn't what we would call "life." I have, however, been mired in this problem for almost ten years."

"Ten years! Have you been here for such a long time? What kind of pain and disease do you have?"

"Being lonely is what causes my suffering. Otherwise, I would have gotten the hell out of here a long time ago."

"What you are expressing is understandable to me. Nobody in their right mind would do this unless it was absolutely necessary."

"Just like us."

"I won't ever stay here; you can be sure of that. I'll pack my things and leave here as soon as I start to feel a little better. I don't even turn to look back."

"Naturally, provided that the big sister consents. If not, you will be stuck here for a very long time."

"What the hell are you saying? Should the big sister agree to let us get out of here?"

"As soon as you stepped foot on this place, you became subject to the regulations that had been established by the big sister. If you disobey any of these rules in any way, you will have the opportunity to witness hell firsthand."

"You've got to be kidding me, right?"

"In the beginning, I didn't take this issue seriously. But I figured out what was going on very soon."

"What makes them call her the big sister, then? What distinguishing traits does she possess?"

"Because of the position she has found, she was awarded this title. If I tell you that many people consider her to be a saint, you won't believe me!"

"Are you kidding?"

""No way." It is inconceivable how much they obey her around here. They even make vows for her!"

"Oh my God, if I had realized I would face such a circumstance, I never would have left that damned camp. There, at least, I would die with dignity and honor."

"It's still not too late. You can leave as long as your name is not on the list. But it is better not to do this."

"Why?"

"Because you cannot go too far from here. In addition to the chilly, windy, and stormy conditions, there's always the chance of running into that supernatural creature hiding in the mountains."

"Which creature are you talking about?"

"The locals think this creature is a cross between an animal and a primitive man! However, no one has yet been able to provide evidence for its existence."

"I have heard Yeti and Bigfoot legends. But I had no idea the extent of these superstitions extended all the way to here."

"There is undoubtedly something frightening up there, but not in the way that most people would imagine."

"Can you explain more precisely?"

"I think that the big sister has sent someone in that direction to look for the runaways and the rebels."

"When the snow melted the year before, they discovered the remains of numerous bodies that had horribly deteriorated up there. The bodies had been up there for quite some time. On their bodies were wounds and injuries that could not have been caused by the wild creatures and carrion eaters."

"How are you so sure of this? Have you seen the deceased individuals?"

"No, several people came from the city to investigate this issue. I heard from one of them."

"So you mean I got stuck between the devil and the deep blue sea? Is that right?"

"If I tell you to do something, you should wait until your treatment is over. Then you won't have to worry about going anywhere."

"And what if I do not get treated?"

"In this kind of situation, patients are usually left with their families to spend their last days with them. If you don't have someone to take care of you, they will take you downstairs and get you ready for the last symphony. Do you get what I'm saying?"

"Obviously. I've already looked at those crypts."

"So, sooner than I anticipated, you were aware of the situation here!"

"Leaving these remarks aside, how long does the typical treatment session last here?"

"First and foremost, it depends on your own health, but the big sister and her advisory board will make the final decision."

"If that is the case, then I do not have the freedom to choose."

"You're right, more or less. In addition, the manner in which patients are treated differs greatly from that of the outside world. From the big sister's perspective, the health of the body is impossible without spiritual purification."

"These are all nonsense and demagogic words."

"Maybe so, but we all have to precisely follow her orders. If not, she will put us through the wringer."

"Let's talk turkey. I'm ready to put my chest in front of the bullet, but I won't be a prisoner of this witch's wishes."

"What you're saying makes sense to me. However, you are not required to agree with him wholeheartedly. You can simply pretend to do what I do. In this way, you won't give her a reason to get angry. Then, after some time, you will be able to resume your normal life. Of course, on the condition that you won't have gone insane by then!"

"I appreciate your encouraging words very much. I, however, do not belong to the group of people who would accept such humiliation."

The old man gave a thoughtful smile and said:

"It is completely clear."

Then he looked at me thoughtfully.

I continued:

"Are you offended by my words?"

"Absolutely not."

"Then why did you suddenly begin to think?"

"I just remembered something."

"Go ahead and tell me what's going through your brain, but please be truthful with me."

"To be honest, I had a strange dream that kept my mind busy this morning. I really want to know what you think about it."

"It is best to describe your dream to a dream interpreter. After all, I give these remarks absolutely no value. I believe that all of these problems stem from illusions and superstitions."

"You are right, but my dream is somehow related to you. That's why I really like to tell you about it. I promise I won't take up much of your time."

I didn't care what he had to say about it, and I assumed that his main objective was to catch my attention. But refusing this sweet and lovely old man's request seemed impolite. He got very happy and continued more enthusiastically:

"I had a dream that I was feeling very ill and was lying in bed. The dream was very vivid. It felt like the moment of my passing had finally arrived. Simultaneously, the door to the room opened, and a figure that was strikingly similar to you materialized on the threshold of the door. He remained there for a short while and gazed at me in an odd manner at that time. After that, he walked into the room. It appeared as though he was floating in the air with his gait. A strange and lovely light also streamed behind him like a waterfall. He approached me with a cheery expression on his face and inquired about how I was doing. I was unable to express any reaction to him as I stared at him for several moments since I was so taken aback by the spiritual and magnificent appeal that he exuded. It was exactly as though Christ had materialized in front of me. After I felt better, I pointed to my suffering and sick body and said: I'm feeling this, as you can see. I'm waiting for death to arrive so that it can free me from all of this anguish. He placed his hand on my body very slowly and gently while saying, "Don't worry; you'll be fine soon." Then you feel as if you've been reborn. He then gave me a forehead kiss and added: Wait for the signs; that's all. I wanted to ask him what sign it was that he meant when he said he vanished from my vision like dust and left no trace. It is difficult to believe, I know. But this morning, when I saw you, I experienced an odd sensation, as if my dream had been interpreted."

"You were only having a dream, old man. You are far too intelligent to be influenced by such little matters."

"Perhaps you're right. But I just can't get it off my head."

"There is no doubt that there's something within you that has had such a profound impact on me. I think you'll grow into a wonderful person one day, a person who affects social change.'

"Oh, Old man, you are so generous. But it would be better to do something about this fucking place first. We would be inspired to take on more challenging tasks in the future if we could make some improvements in this area."

"I concur with you. Furthermore, I still don't know your name and address."

"I have no unique name or address. You can call me Nicholas simply and swiftly, or more precisely, call me Nicholas Mortimer."

"This is a name I believe I've heard before. Could you please tell me where you're from?"

"Before the war, I resided in Philadelphia. My heritage, though, originates from South Carolina."

"Therefore, why did you dress like a northerner? Maybe you are covering your tracks."

"Despite the fact that I was born in the South, my ideas and perspectives have led me to the North. What about you? Do you like Northerners?"

"To be really honest, I don't have much faith in these fronts."

"Does that mean you don't care about the future of your country?"

"As I previously stated, I was imprisoned here for years prior to the start of the war. I mean."

"Just tell me something: Are you in favor of or opposed to slavery?"

"Naturally, I am against No one should, in my opinion, be subjected to oppression or discrimination because of the color of his skin."

"So we are both on the same side of the front. Aren't we?'

"Don't stress over this. I've always been a liberal and a fan of freedom. Now let's enjoy ourselves and have a drink."

"Do you have alcohol with you?"

The old man said proudly:

"I also have the good kind."

"Would you mind telling me where you acquired it?"

"It is not a challenging task. You just have to grease some people's palms a little. Of course, cautiously."

"So you can have a good time here as well."

"Why not! If a good opportunity comes tonight, I will show you something that will surprise you."

"Now, take a few sips of this drink to feel better."

We heard someone's footsteps ascending the stairs at that very moment.

The old man quickly snatched the bottle out of my grasp and tucked it away beneath his coat. He asked me to go back to bed and pretend to sleep after he went back to his seat.

When the door opened, and one of the big sisters entered the room with a tray of food, I hadn't even gotten under the covers.

The elderly man instantly stood up and grabbed the tray from her. Nuns were reportedly forbidden from visiting the sick except when they were in need of assistance or medical attention or when they were in their final moments.

The people who were employed as laborers actually completed the majority of the job, similar to the harsh and unattractive man who admitted me to the monastery. The breakfast, by the way, was just as bad as I thought it would be. It was so bad that the meager army rations looked like gourmet food.

Like the night before, they handed me a glass of cold milk and some black, essentially stale bread. There was also a bowl of unpleasant-tasting soup next to it.

The dish was devoid of garlic. Evidently, they checked to make sure I wasn't a monster or a vampire and that I wasn't there with the goal of stealing their souls.

I had only taken a few nibbles when I started to feel nauseous and stopped eating the remaining food.

The old man gave his bottle of wine to me and said:

"The big sister refers to this dirt as "healthy food!" I assure you that a dog will become enraged if you provide it with this garbage. This explains why our mortality rate is so high."

"So what about fresh fruits and vegetables? Do you mean to imply that these are the only things that can count toward our food ration?"

"Do you understand what you're saying? This is the best food you can find in this fucking place. Thank God we can sometimes get something from the villagers and pilgrims because if we couldn't, we would have died of hunger."

"Are you kidding? What does it have to do with the fact that people come here to make vows and meet their needs?"

"Go to them and ask. Now, if you don't mind, I'll get to work. I hope my words didn't bore you."

"Absolutely not. Thanks a lot for coming to see me. I hope we can hang out more and get to know each other better."

The old man gave me a warm and friendly smile and said:
"Sure"

Then he left the room, leaving me alone with lots of things to think about.

I have to say that his encouraging words and presence had a big effect on me, and I wasn't as sad and hopeless as I was before.

At the same time, his words made me have more doubts and questions and made me want to learn more about this place and the people who live there.

Undoubtedly, I had tough and draining days ahead of me when my tenacity and sincerity challenged me and put me in the crucible in a new way. But I also vowed to myself that I would never again be put in that predicament, even if doing so meant running afoul of the big sister and other people in charge of this place and the helpless people who live there.

I was thinking and dreaming about these things when I suddenly got a bad burning feeling in my stomach, and then I had a bad stomachache and colic.

Of course, it didn't come as a surprise. Even strong, healthy people had a hard time digesting food like that, so imagine how hard it was for a sick person with a weak stomach like me.

It might take me a week or two to fully get used to this new situation.

I put on my uniform, which was still damp, after I felt better and left the monastery to get some fresh air.

That morning, there was no more wind, storm, or snowstorm in the huge expanse of the mountains, and there was a stillness that seemed to have sprung straight out of a dream.

The sky was clear and blue as far as the eye could see, and it was perfectly flat. It was like someone had put a huge, blank canvas in front of me, ready for me to paint the most accurate picture of nature I could think of.

Furthermore, a pleasant and refreshing breeze was blowing.

I took a closer look at my surroundings, which had found a new incarnation in the light of day while I was taking in this uplifting and lovely weather.

The monastery was constructed in a location in the mountains where it was totally surrounded by nature. In reality, it was the perfect location to keep an eye on the neighborhood because nearly no movement was hidden from the residents' view of the fortress.

If you saw this structure from a distance, you might think it was a fortified fortress.

In any case, this location's unique geography allowed me to both appreciate this place's beauty and get a greater sense of my surroundings.

At the same time, I couldn't help but notice how lively the mountain region was. When I really looked, I saw a large group of reindeer coming down from a very steep cliff.

At the bottom of the valley, where this rock stopped, there was a river that was constantly roaring due to the gradual melting of the snow.

I was truly amazed by the beauty and splendor of this animal, which had found a unique and fascinating way to live in the wild world around it.

Only the violence and cruelty of people could have stopped this beautiful animal from being so proud and determined.

While I was completely absorbed in looking at these sights and praising them, someone came up behind me and put his hand on my shoulder and gave me a friendly greeting.

When I turned around, I saw a relatively young man who appeared to be in a lot of pain and was quite frail; in comparison, I appeared to be in good health and in a good mood in front of him! It was pretty obvious that he had deteriorated to this state as a direct result of the severity of the disease as well as the persistent hunger that he had endured. He was exactly like the majority of people who were forced to travel to this location. After saying hello, he pointed to the scene in front of us and said, with a sad face,

"I was just like you in the beginning. I thought This is the paradise that was promised!" But after a while, I got used to it all and got bored with it. The only thing that never gets old is the pain that scratches your soul from morning to night. I promise you; I don't want to let you down. I just want you to face the truth as soon as possible and know what's in store for you. You might be able to avoid this danger in some way."

"You thought I wouldn't know these things on my own. As soon as I walked into this place and met the big sister, I knew what was going on. If I could go somewhere else, I wouldn't stay here for a second."

"We're all pretty much the same. I just hope that as long as I'm still alive, I'll have another chance to experience the good life and, more importantly, freedom."

"Don't be afraid that we can't get through this. We just need the courage to stand up to force and not give in to anything.'

"I think you're right. Just don't say them in front of the big sister. If you do, you won't be able to see these simple and small things."

"I hear the same thing from everyone here. Does that mean you're so scared of her and that she has so much power over you?"

He gestured and urged me to slightly lower my voice. Then he led me to a quiet nook and remarked:

"This woman's power lies in the ignorance of people who believe in her. If she has a problem with someone, it will bring him a catastrophe that will make him wish for his own death a thousand times per day."

I acknowledge:

"What you said is accurate, but this is not an excuse to do nothing. Such prejudices and narrowmindedness are currently vanishing and being erased. If you had knowledge of the outside world, you would realize the changes that have occurred."

"You are correct. However, the majority of these alterations and adjustments happened elsewhere, not in this hellhole where people continue to live in a medieval manner."

"How is it even feasible to accomplish such a thing? Is it even possible that they have strung barbed wire all around this area?"

"No. Just because of the environment, there has been no communication between the locals and the outside world.

Because of their beliefs and prejudices, they stand in the way of development and enlightenment.'

"What about the big sister? Is she from around here?"

"I'm not sure. She speaks with a slightly different accent than the others. In any case, you'd better pay attention to what I say and stop fighting with her so much. She will make your life miserable if you do."

"Oh my god, I can't believe you are so scared of a frail and skinny nun."

"It seems like you didn't get what I was saying. It's not just that the big sister is a problem. What matters is how badly she affects other people's minds, especially the locals, people who live in the area, and the illiterate ones, those who don't know how to read or write. She only needs to ask one of them for something, and after that, she can have anything she wants. Then you'll see what they do for her alone. It's like she's holding a divine command!"

"My God, you mean things are so bad here?"

"Absolutely. If I tell you what horrible things she has done and the catastrophes she has caused, you will most likely not believe me."

"The question now is why my superior officer did not discuss any of this with me. He has an in-depth familiarity with this location."

"Perhaps he really was clueless about everything. Perhaps he had the intention of getting rid of you in this manner."

"What exactly did you intend to say this?"

Before he answered my question, a monastery servant approached us with a frown on her face and said that the big sister wanted to see him as soon as possible. They most likely intended to warn him not to get any closer to me because they were concerned that the blasphemous things I said could contaminate his mind.

As I walked around the monastery and thought about these things, I ran into the kind old man who had stopped me from sleeping in the morning.

He was sitting in the corner of the wall and enjoying the winter sun.

When he saw me, he called me over with great excitement and said, "Come here, my friend; come and get as much as you can out of this life-giving glory." We might not be able to see the sun's color for a long time.

I also joined him willingly and with a lot of enthusiasm, just like a lover who rushes to his loved one when he or she asks him or her out. I have to be honest and say that this man's charm and charisma made me want to be with him.

I didn't know much about him, though. He didn't even tell me his name and his family.

When I asked him about this, he answered quickly:

"Joe, you can call me Joe." Enough already!"

So I could get to know him better, I kept going:

"Well, Joe, tell me where you're from."

He answered me as he was lighting his pipe:

"I'm from the north. More specifically, I was born somewhere close to Minnesota. But I wasn't one of those people who spent too much time in one place."

"May I ask what you do for a living?"

"I've been everywhere and done everything, from looking for gold to carrying things. I also did a lot of things that, when I think of them now, make me feel embarrassed and ashamed."

I asked:

"Do you have a wife and kids or not?" because I was still interested."

The old man seemed a little upset by this question as if it made him think of bad or upsetting things. After some hesitation and thought, he said:

"I was much younger than you when I got married and started a family." His tone and face showed his pain and sadness. I was happy and in love for a while, but then I lost my wife while she was pregnant. Our baby was born dead, which was very sad. After that happened, I couldn't live with anyone else."

"I feel terrible to hear that. I'm sorry to bring these things up again. I only asked because I was interested."

"No problem, young man. Anyway, I always remember these things."

"Do you have someone in your family who can help you and take care of you?"

"I only have one younger sister, and she lives in Arkansas. I haven't heard from her in years, so that's not a surprise."

"Is she aware that you're here or not? At first, I sent her several letters in which I told her everything. But she never got back to me."

"Well, maybe she didn't get the letter."

"Maybe so. It's possible that she didn't want to date me. We didn't get along very well, even more so after she got married."

"Why?"

"Her husband wasn't all that interesting. I have no idea what she saw in that man that made her fall in love with him."

"Anyway, we fought and argued a few times until my sister's patience ran out, and she told me in no uncertain terms to get out of her life."

"So it's not too strange that you haven't heard back from her yet. There are, however, different possibilities. Maybe your sister's husband got the letters, but he didn't tell your sister about them."

"I had also thought about this. I couldn't do anything special, though. I could find out more about her if I had someone else."

"Don't worry. I may be able to help you with this."

"Seriously?"

"Some people out there have been kind to me and have been there for me many times. I just need to figure out how to get in touch with them."

"You are very nice. I hope I can make up for it one day."

"Don't mention it. Now tell me how you came here."

"Did you lose your way?"

"I wish that was the case. Sadly, illness and disability brought me and most of the other people who live here to this hellhole. I did my best, of course, to find a way to be settled in life."

"I should admit that I lived in misery and poverty for a while. I had to do stupid and pointless things just to get a piece of bread and not die. But as time went on, I got so weak that I could no longer work and make money easily.

This kept going on until one day, by chance, I ran into a friend and former coworker who was in charge of a nursery room. He was the one who told me where this place was. I don't know if he did it out of kindness or to hurt me."

"I'm sorry to bring these things back up. You must be very sad when you remember those days."

"No. I only miss the times I didn't get to enjoy. I wish I was a little smarter about how I did things."

"We've all been through these things. It's important to keep trying hard and not give up on our dreams and goals."

"I agree with you. But at my age, hope is like a dream that keeps getting smaller and smaller."

"Let's not talk about these things. I really want to know what you think about this war."

"What's your point of view?"

"Please don't get it wrong. I don't want to start a political category; I just want to know which side you agree with the most."

"Does it really matter?"

"Do you mean to say that you are unconcerned with the fate of our nation or its future leaders?"

"Now consider a scenario in which the northerners triumph. What unique changes do you anticipate occurring?"

"I have no doubt that we will be heading in the right direction if Abraham Lincoln wins the presidency. Have you ever listened to his speeches?"

"No. I only read a couple of his articles that dealt with liberty and social justice."

"You must be aware of the outstanding speech he delivered in Gettysburg. Many people regained hope for the future of this nation following that speech."

"I concur that he holds admirable values and views. However, do not undervalue the forces in opposition. They won't be so easily defeated, in my opinion."

"I didn't say that, to be clear. But I have no doubt that we will ultimately triumph."

"Why are you so certain?"

"It is because we uphold the ideal values and standards that ensure our nation's prosperity and pride. You disagree, don't you?"

"Not at all. Every wise person understands that the end of slavery marks the beginning of this nation's progress and development. However, winning this conflict cannot in and of itself provide for anything. In my opinion, the constitution is the most crucial issue. This needs to be done very carefully, taking into consideration all factors, or else all of their efforts and sacrifices will be in vain."

"You are correct. Our freedom is guaranteed by the constitution. Every country has the same situation. I hope to live long enough to witness the realization of this goal."

"What do you think about Andrew Johnson? I believe that he is capable of taking on a leadership role."

"He has done a lot for this country's future. But he doesn't have Abraham Lincoln's charm and charisma. Lincoln is the only person I think can help us get what we want and what we dream of."

"I hope what you say is true. But we have a long way to go before we get to that point. Putting these words aside, do you think the war could spread here?"

"It's not so impossible, even though it doesn't matter much to people like me."

"What do you mean?!"

"We haven't got much to lose. Death itself can be a blessing."

"Don't say this, my friend, because there is always something to lose or regret. Even when it seems like all the doors are closed, and you don't have any hope or reason to keep going."

"I believe you are correct. In any event, I wish that the specter of war would not linger here. Whether it is north or south, I don't care. None of them should get this far."

"You'll probably find this upsetting, but there are members of both sides' ranks who would commit any crime or shameful behavior. I don't worry too much about myself. I really don't want to see these individuals suffer any longer. These people's plight is enough. Don't you agree?"

The old man didn't say anything incorrect. Such scenes were frequently seen by me.

Even those who were admired and respected by others and appeared incapable of committing cruel or inhumane acts may do so. It serves as the catalyst for his spiritual and mental collapse. In such circumstances, people begin acting in ways that are incompatible with human dignity.

But there are people who want to do these things, and the war gives them a chance to do what they want without hiding it.

While we were talking about this and giving each other our opinions, one of the servants came up to us and told us in a harsh, commanding voice to clear the snow from the area.

I was shocked and questioned:

"Why do we do this?" These issues are your responsibilities, right?

He said with a grimace:

"Because that is what the big sister requested. Do you now understand?"

I responded by acting even more brazen and reckless, asking:

"Are we her servants that she commands and prohibits us so much?" After all, how are we supposed to shovel all this snow when we are in such poor health?"

"This is no longer about me. We are all required to obey any directives from the big sister issues."

"Does that imply you are listening to her with your eyes and ears closed? Even if it goes against logic and reason."

"You have no right to speak that way about her."

"Does that imply that she is faultless?"

"You are not qualified to interrogate the big sister."

"So, who is capable?"

"I don't want to talk about this anymore. Get up and do what I told you to do. If you don't, you'll have a lot of problems."

"For example, what do you want to do? Do you want to impale me?"

He didn't say a word to me, and he went back to the monastery, angry and confused. After he left, the old man gave me some advice and scolded me for acting so rudely and inconsiderately.

In response, I said sarcastically:

"If there was a decent person to stand up to this person's threats, she would not have dared to go this far."

He said in a grumpy tone:

"Don't hurry, my friend. You just got here, so you don't yet know how things work here. In the beginning, I felt the same as you. But I quickly realized that we couldn't do anything special. You can't talk to these people because they are so rigid and shortsighted."

"Did you notice how he responded to you? Every single one of them is the same as this one."

"For example, what do you want to do? Did you think you could change these people?"

"No, not really. But we can at least change ourselves."

"I don't know what you're thinking, but I don't have the guts to talk to this person. Don't worry about this. I just don't want things to get worse for us."

"You don't have to explain yourself. I'll give it some thought."

"Don't get mad, please. If I say something, it's just to help you. This person is a lot riskier than you might think. I worry that you will get hurt one day."

"Don't be afraid. I am not that weak and awkward to be scared of such people."

"Right here is where you're wrong. When you're up against someone whose power comes from other people's ignorance, bigotry, or lack of knowledge, you should move carefully and cautiously. If you don't, you'll fall into a well that doesn't end."

"To put it more simply, you're not just up against the big sister and a few holy, strict nuns here. In reality, you are dealing with a lot of common, illiterate people who are easily angered and do horrible, crazy things."

"I get what you're saying. But it's hard for me to accept something like this. It feels like I'm giving up my soul."

"I know what you're saying. Do you really know how I feel about what's going on? Believe me, this woman has embarrassed me over and over again. I just want a miracle to happen so I can get rid of her."

"Old man, there is no miracle. No one else can help us but ourselves."

"You're correct. Let's skip these words and go shovel the snow. In any case, it's better than being lazy and not making a choice. But don't stress yourself out too much."

"What? You think I can't do something so simple?"

"It's not as easy as you might think. In other words, you don't have enough strength to do it."

"I'm willing to bet with you that I can shovel all the snow in the area in 30 minutes, making it as smooth and clean as my palm."

"Quit it. This is not at all possible."

"Why don't you take the bet if you are so sure?"

"I don't want you to get into trouble. At least give yourself a few days to get back on your feet. Then you can show off your strength and power."

"Right now, I'm ready. Don't be afraid!"

"Now that you're being so insistent, I'll bet you ten dollars."

"No, twenty."

"You don't think I sat on the treasure, do you? I could hardly save this $10."

"I mean, after all these years, you were here, but you couldn't save a big sum of money for yourself."

"How was it possible?"

"Didn't you say that you knew the people here? You could make a bet with them."

"What for?! I have to have something in my bag that will make them want to talk to me. Aside from that, the big sister doesn't let us make money this way."

"She should be cursed. I don't know what I did wrong to deserve this person's anger."

"You just had bad luck, friend, just like me."

"So, ten dollars will do. Anyway, it doesn't take long."

"Let's see, my friend. No matter what happens, I will win."

"How come?!"

"While you're working hard and getting sweaty, I'll just sit here and enjoy the morning sun. More than ten dollars are worth it."

"I don't worry about money. I just want to prove myself to you."

"I just know that you are stupid and stubborn and don't care about yourself at all. Just make sure no one figures out that we made a bet, or we will get in a lot of trouble."

"Now roll up your sleeves and get to work. I want to see what you have to offer."

I said with confidence:

"I'll surprise you."

The old man smiled and said:

"I haven't won a bet in a long time." I'm glad you gave me this chance."

He was right to be so sure that he would win. It didn't take me long to realize what a stupid and incorrect thing I had said. I didn't realize how hard it would be to do this, and it put a lot of stress on my sick body.

In other words, I couldn't do anything about it. But my pride wouldn't let me just accept that I had lost.

While I was working hard and sweating, the old man was relaxing in a corner and enjoying the sun and the beautiful natural scenery.

When I took a break from work to rest, he looked triumphantly at my tired and sweaty face and asked:

"Do you feel like conceding defeat right now, or are you sticking to your word?"

I was unable to continue since I was so out of breath. However, I refrained from admitting my evident weakness and incapability. Thus, I responded:

"There is still some time left. Just be patient while I catch my breath and recharge before I show you my strength."

The old man gave me a suspicious look and said:

"I'm not in a hurry, my friend. But it looks like you won't be able to finish the job."

"So don't worry about this bet, and don't give it any more thought."

"By saying this, he gave me even more energy and made me more determined to get over my physical weakness and disability. But I couldn't handle this task, so I had to leave it to him."

"The only good thing about it was that for a few moments, even though they were short, it made me feel good and polished my soul a little."

While I was taking a break, the old man got up and went to that pile of snow that I couldn't move.

At first, I thought he wanted me to finish the work I had started but not finished.

He did something I didn't expect him to do, which surprised me. It made me happier and helped me feel less tired at the same time.

The old man was very excited about making a snowman as he thought back to his childhood.

I truly did not anticipate that the interior of this ancient tree would all of a sudden give off such a warm and invigorating sensation, which would then have an effect on the dreary environment that was all around me.

The big sister was observing our every action from behind the window at the time. We both knew this very well. But none of us paid her any particular attention, as if she weren't even there.

The big sister was unable to accept such behavior from the patients and residents of the monastery and was vehemently opposed to anything that brought about the so-called excitement of the outside world there. Thus, if she found anyone in violation of the regulations, he would be subject to harsh punishment.

Before telling the rest of the story, it's best to give a short description of this kind of punishment. This will help you understand how cruel this place was.

I heard that the simplest kind of torture was to lock someone up in a room that looked like a mausoleum from the Middle Ages.

People who were given this sort of punishment were forced to endure mental anguish for an undetermined amount of time until they admitted their error and expressed regret. If not, they would endure cruel physical torture.

I think that the big sister had support from influential and powerful people, or else she wouldn't be so rude and bold. But in reality, it is the ignorance and indifference of others that make it possible for these people to get what they want and keep thinking stupid things.

The big sister did not think we would react in such a way. She thought that her charm and scary look would soon be enough to make us give in to her and go back to our crypts with our heads down, just like people who have done something bad and then felt bad about it.

Because of this, she just stood there and looked at us for a while without doing anything else. But finally, she couldn't take it anymore, and she told us in a very harsh, reprimanding way to stop this childish behavior and not disturb the peace and quiet of others.

Then she gave the servant the order to destroy our snowman as fast as possible!

I'm telling the truth; you can trust that. I had never encountered a woman with such prejudice and inflexible beliefs as this one. She couldn't even bear to wait for the snowman to melt as the weather warmed up gradually. It appeared as though something among the snowman's crystals and frozen particles frightened her and made her throne of power shake.

It was highly offensive and discriminatory behavior that demonstrated the extent of her ignorance as well as her underlying wickedness. But I was not in a position to give her a response that was appropriate given the circumstances at the time.

The big sister feared that people would notice our actions as an example and begin to doubt her commitment to her spirituality. She also discussed harsher sanctions for us because of this, such as depriving us of one meal and locking us in our rooms for a whole 24 hours!

None of us found these punishments to be infuriating or intolerable. The old man wanted to share some food with me that he had already stored for himself.

So there was nothing wrong with this. The only thing that made me feel bad was being locked in that cold and mostly dark room, but not as much as the big sister thought. But this wasn't the only thing I was going to get into trouble for.

I had to go to the bathroom because they made me! You must be wondering what's so bad about going to the bathroom.

So, it's clear that nothing is wrong with it. I should say that I needed it a lot. I didn't like being naked in front of other people, though.

The big sister told the man with the ugly face and hunched back not to take his eyes off me for even a second.

It was clear that she wanted to hurt me even more. If she didn't, why did she do this?

I was ready to be locked in my room for several days and nights with nothing to eat, but I didn't want to see this person while I was getting naked and taking a bath.

Don't make a snap judgment. I don't want to say how repulsed and disgusted I was by his appearance. I was absolutely annoyed and tortured by the way he looked and behaved.

He appeared to be looking at my naked body as though I were a young and intoxicated girl standing in front of him. I feared that he would suddenly lose control of himself and come at me like a ravenous monster at any minute. This was considered a type of sexual harassment.

I repeatedly requested that he face the opposite direction and leave me alone. Not only did he disregard my request, but he also dumped several buckets of cold water into the bathtub to aggravate me further.

It's okay to bring up a topic here that has nothing to do with the narrative but is nonetheless important to know. Virgin girls, nuns, and workers for churches and monasteries were prohibited from using hot water for personal hygiene during the Middle Ages. Considering that they thought hot water stimulated their libido and drove them deeper into immorality!

However, it wasn't a rule that everyone had to abide by. Such rigorous and strict regulations were only enforced in certain religious settings. The passage of time clearly demonstrated that these excessive behaviors not only have no positive effects, but also lead to numerous issues and sexual aberrations.

In the meantime, another crew member took my clothing and placed it all in the oven without asking me a question.

Lucky for me, none of them were important or valuable enough for me to feel bad about losing them, except for the clothes, which had a religious and holy feeling.

I was especially interested in this cloth because I had worn it in several essential battles where it made a difference.

Even though it was dirty and old and the fabric was falling apart, I was happy and proud to wear and keep it.

Instead, they gave me a pair of spotless garments that did not differ all that much from the ones worn by the prisoners.

They then shaved my head, akin to beating the wool off lambs. Just having my hands and feet restrained was enough to make me appear insane.

I wished at that time that I had been committed to jail or a mental hospital rather than living in such a place. At least I had more freedom of thought and action because I was not subject to these onerous and strict rules.

Let us move on. I was disheartened when I returned to my room with this new head and condition and observed my new face in the mirror. At that time, I had the impression of someone who had resigned to ignominy and shame after sacrificing his soul in the land of ignorance and darkness.

I was dreaming about these things when I heard a coughing fit from the other room.

I had not yet had the opportunity to become acquainted with the other residents and patients. Although it was apparent what to anticipate, pain and anguish, despondency and disillusionment, a sense of emptiness and oblivion, and, ultimately, death was the inescapable legacies of this location and its governing petrification.

However, slowly, a small quantity of light and hope came through, which I could see the following day.

Just as my old friend emerged from his tight cocoon, he poured new life into his body and ours by building that snowman.

They had ruthlessly smashed and trampled our snowman. Although he was only here for a brief time, the impression that he left on any of us will never be forgotten.

***

Around noon, the big sister sent someone to insultingly and shockingly ask me to go to her room. It was like she was calling one of her humble workers or subordinates.

I took longer to go to her room to make it plain that I was afraid I had to disagree with her commands and had no qualms about disobeying them.

This, in my opinion, was the least I could do in the face of all her constant orders and warnings, as well as her deaf and blind followers.

When I entered her room, she was taking notes from various sacred writings and books while seated at a rather large table with an oak-colored finish.

I waited quietly for a few moments for her to finish her task before I spoke again. However, she did not pay even the slightest attention to me, as if I were not there.

She was trying to show me that she does not think much of me and sees me as one of her subordinates and servants, but she did not realize that I knew what she meant by what she was doing.

While I waited, I looked at the room's corners and the throne of her authority.

It met my expectations. The corners of the room were adorned with non-artistically valuable religious images and symbols that primarily reflected the ideas and opinions of the big sister and her followers.

The only thing that caught my eye and piqued my interest was a large rack of primarily religious books. Nevertheless, there were also some excellent and valuable works among them.

It was clear that the big sister and the others were uninterested in these projects.

In this respect, there was a great deal of dust on their covers, as opposed to religious books and writings, which appeared to be relatively clean and organized. Thank God at least that they did not destroy them.

At the same time, my gaze was drawn to some strange devices in another corner of the room that resembled torture and confession devices.

Seeing such things set off alarm bells in my ears, increasing my skepticism and concern for my future.

There were definitely hard days ahead of me, filled with anxiety and inflammation, unless I changed my behavior and interaction with the big sister and tolerated her a little. Otherwise, I'd be slaughtered like a helpless lamb.

In such a situation, the best course of action was to pretend to listen to her and stop bothering her.

It seemed like a simple chore that I could perform effortlessly. However, I did not intend to cover up and please such a person. This was opposed to the beliefs and standards that I had always followed, and because of it, I faced a lot of trouble.

In my opinion, the sister represented prejudice and intellectual mediocrity. When such people have political influence and authority, their only contributions to society are destruction and backwardness.

If this happens, their thoughts will spread around the world and cause terrible things to happen.

The big sister was much inferior to what we imagined. But she was able to force her absurd and irrational demands on us because she was powerful and influential enough.

In general, it's hard to live with these kinds of people, and it's impossible to talk to them or do anything productive with them.

In other words, they only accept and like people who don't openly disagree with them and who act in a way that is consistent with their customs. If they don't, they will face their anger and hatred, and at best, they will be kicked out of their group.

If they go beyond this and try to find enlightenment, they will be called blasphemers and atheists, and they will mess up our lives.

It took hundreds of years for thinkers and intellectuals to be able to break through some of the rigidity and bigotry and open doors to the rest of the world. But it doesn't look like it will be possible to get completely free of this opium.

The only thing that can be done is to limit this group's power and influence as much as possible and not let them get involved in people's personal and political lives; otherwise, all of these accomplishments will fade and be forgotten over time.

Let's move on. The big sister was so quiet and didn't pay attention to me that I finally gave up and asked her in a not-very polite way:

"Did you have anything to do with me, sister?"

She turned her head right away and glared at me. Her actions made me feel like I had done something very bad in front of her.

Then, in a harsh voice, she said:

"I've been waiting for you for ten minutes." Can you tell me where you were?

I answered calmly:

"I was taking care of my personal affairs. I have a lot of things to do!"

The big sister continued with more anger:

"This behavior is not appropriate for a soldier like you! You should be ashamed of yourself."

I answered very frankly:

"This is not a barracks, and you are not a commander here. So don't fuss."

She never expected to hear such a word. My boldness and recklessness had reached such a level that it would deeply frighten a person like her.

I will never forget the special expression on her face at that moment.

She gave me a skewed face as she regarded me. She felt as though something unusual and perplexing was in front of her.

I anticipated that she would launch a defensive attack in this circumstance. Surprisingly, though, it did not take place.

She remained silent for a few moments and did not say anything.

It was evident that she was tremendously agitated and restless on the inside and was looking for a suitable moment to slaughter me. However, she displayed an unexpected display of tenderness and kindly requested that I sit in the chair in front of her and listen to what she had to say.

I knew exactly what she wanted to do. She wanted to tell me what to do and preach to me again. More could not be expected of such individuals!

I didn't give a damn about what she said, and deep down, I laughed at her. But it wasn't in my best interest to stand against her more than what I had done so far.

At the time, there was no reason for me to enrage this person and turn them against myself. So, I politely and humbly agreed to what she asked me to do.

As soon as I sat down in the chair, I had the sudden realization that, in terms of its size, it was not very proportional to the table that was in front of me.

It appeared as though the legs of this chair had been purposefully cut down to a shorter length than usual in order to make anyone who stood in front of the big sister feel inferior and small.

It's as though we were invited to be in the presence of a renowned princess or queen who didn't allow anyone into her personal space.

She proceeded to preach to me and give me some advice, just as I had anticipated.

I also responded with respect. Thus, she became enraged and uttered insulting and humiliating words, which, under normal circumstances, would make me angry and upset and prompt me to respond and fight back.

But at the time, I was smart and kept from getting into more verbal fights with her.

Contrary to my expectations, this strategy was ineffective. It enraged her even more than before!

This action was interpreted by the big sister as an act of derision and disrespect directed toward her, and as a result, she hurled a number of slurs and other meaningless statements at me.

Again, I managed to keep my composure and refrain from saying anything that may have made the situation even more precarious. However, she did not stop and continued to say things that, on the one hand, made me laugh and, on the other hand, made me feel sad.

In general, she thought that all of my actions and behavior were impudent, lacking any sense of shame, and going against the norms that were established for this place.

I gave her some time to speak her mind before I responded to any of her statements. Then I calmly asked:

"What did I do wrong to make you so angry?"

She responded with a bewildered expression:

"What else did you want to happen?! This morning, we requested that you clear the area of snow. We also completed this swiftly. Didn't we?"

"Of course. But in a manner that caused discomfort and deprived others of comfort."

"I don't get what you're saying. Are you upset that we made a condition?"

"I know nothing about this situation. I'll take care of it later, of course!"

"Then why are you so upset?"

"First of all, why did you make that stupid snowman?" Then there's the noise and disruption you caused by doing it. Your laughter is so loud that it can be heard on the other side of the mountain. "You really made us feel embarrassed."

"I am very sorry. You talk as if the sky is falling. "What could be wrong with making a snowman?!"

"Maybe it is ridiculous and unimportant from your point of view, but this kind of behavior is not suitable for such a place." "After all, it causes confusion of the mind and spreads corruption and moral unrest."

"Oh my God! This is the first time I've heard of someone fighting joy and laughter."

"You misunderstood. If we were somewhere else, I would not say anything. But here, the situation is different.

"How come? You mean you don't need happiness and laughter here? Do you think only sadness is the priority?

"Of course not." There is nothing wrong with happiness and laughter. It is possible on the condition that it is within the scope of religious obligations. "If not, it will contaminate people's thoughts and minds and serve as the foundation for immorality and corruption."

"Could you please explain what you mean by the word sin?"

"Anything that goes against the Bible's instructions and spiritual teachings"

"However, each individual has their own perspective on how these concerns should be interpreted and comprehended." It's possible that other people don't place the same level of importance and value on the things that you regard as essential and priceless.

"I have nothing to do with others. Here are some laws and values that everyone is obligated to follow without exception."

"Sister, we are getting close to the 20th century. If you had left this place for a while and talked to more people, you would have seen how much the world has changed."

"Contrary to what you may believe, I am very aware of what is happening. So many people would not be slaughtering each other like animals if there were not so much corruption and wickedness."

"It, therefore, turns out that you are mistaken about the essence of this war." Sometimes, in order to achieve peace and freedom, there is no other choice but to take up arms and fight. "If not, the society will degenerate and become backward."

"You cannot justify your sins with these "words."

"Which sin are you talking about?"

"I mean, you want to claim that your hand is not contaminated with anyone else's blood."

"I have never fired a gun on an innocent and defenseless person."

"How do you know who is guilty or innocent? "Are you a religious scholar?"

"What exactly do you mean, sister? You don't have to be religious to understand the distinction between good and bad.

I went on.

"After all, the majority of the things that people are taught by religion to consider sinful and corrupt are the product of the ignorance and prejudice of a group of ignorant people, most of whom do not believe in these things at all." They resort to such rubbish in order to intimidate and mislead the general public."

"If what you say is true, then why are there so many people all over the world who are dependent on it?" Does that imply that every single one of these people is completely ignorant?"

"Big sister, there is nothing wrong with being religious." The issue emerges when someone harms others out of prejudice for his or her own faith and beliefs. Religion has generally spread throughout the world through the use of coercion and the establishment of fear. "Take a good look at some of these books if you don't trust me."

"That's enough.""It is clear that you do not believe at all in the Bible and divine teachings."

"I only trust my own logic and reason. I don't believe in the nonsense that goes back thousands of years."

"Oh, my goodness. I did not think that one day an atheist would walk into this holy place.

"I anticipated that you would have such an opinion of me. Anyone who speaks and behaves contrary to your opinions and beliefs is deemed an infidel by others like you. What do you intend to do now, sister, murder and torment me? I'm sure you are an expert at this."

"There is no need for this." I only expect you to obey our rules. At least try to do that until you are here. Then you can go back to your sinful life!

"How do you know how I lived?"

The big sister gave me a contemptuous look and added:

"A person who has such thoughts and beliefs definitely does not adhere to the customs and morals of society."

"Does that imply, in your perspective, that a person without religious convictions cannot be a decent person?"

The big sister tried to avoid this topic and instead started to say bad things about my superior officer, who had helped me get into the group.

Evidently, the colonel lied when he said that I was a devout Catholic from the same type of individuals that the big sister preferred to be surrounded by.

I had no doubt that he desired my welfare, which is why he told them such a large falsehood. But I hope he will tell the truth so I don't get caught up in the place's ignorance and hatred.

The big sister then requested that I not discuss my polytheistic beliefs with anyone else. I will suffer harsh punishment if I don't.

I questioned her in surprise:

"Why don't you get me out of here right away so you can feel at peace if you are so worried about me?"

The big sister responded in a way that did not at all persuade me.

"Because we have commitments that we must fulfill."

"Please speak a little more clearly so that I can understand what kind of commitments you mean."

"We swore to take care of sick and needy people." "Even those who lost their way."

"But when it comes to me, you're quite rigid and sensitive." In addition to these problems, I believe there is another reason. "Is it not?"

The big sister answered with a little hesitation.

"We have some young nuns here who have recently joined us. You might cause them to slip and go astray. You know what I mean."

"I am sorry to say that, but if they are willing to give up their ideals so readily and commit sin according to your statements, then it is best not to continue down this path. After all, all of this rigour and restraint may entice them even more than before, leading them in the same direction you are concerned about. If you ask me, this kind of asceticism and physical celibacy does not enable the person's soul to be elevated in the least bit in any way, shape, or form.

"You're not saying these things out of kindness, young man." "You're simply looking for your mood."

"It's almost as if we don't understand each other, sister." So, please be honest with me about what you expect from me.

"I just said it!"

"I was referring to the restrictions and rules that you have imposed here." "Can I talk to the other sisters?"

The big sister stated more sternly and authoritatively:

"You have no right to talk to any of the nuns unless I give you permission." You are also not permitted to laugh aloud or make jokes with others. No part of your body should be exposed under any circumstances, with the exception of the face and hands up to the elbows. These rules can only be broken in special and emergency situations."

"Isn't that why we were forced to wear these ugly and irritating clothes?!"

"One of the reasons is this."

After hearing these words, I was both astonished and concerned at the same time. I didn't believe the things the big sister was saying to be true. I felt as though I were seeing a terrible nightmare. With the exception of the most isolated villages and monasteries, which are ignorant of the most recent triumphs of civilization and cultural advancements and are not greatly impacted by them, I thought it was highly doubtful that they would impose all these tight and unreasonable laws and limitations elsewhere.

Her bigotry and sensitivity in these areas were funny and stupid, especially given where we were.

Most of the people who lived in this place were very sick and fought death all day long.

In other words, there was so much sickness and weakness around them that they couldn't even do the most basic things.

In this circumstance, people tend to think less about having sex and handling sexual problems. It implies that they are unable to complete it unless they are forced to do so.

The big sister was so afraid of this problem that she became paranoid and started to believe things that weren't true. She thought that every closeness and interaction between people was because of their sexual and sensual needs and wants.

She talked a little more about this and added at the end:

"I know you weren't expecting such rules here. I must emphasize that we are a unique and unaffiliated community. "Even the Pope has no power or influence in this place."

I responded sarcastically:

"I understand, sister. But, by using these strategies, people's souls cannot find salvation. "I think only greater sin and corruption will result from it."

"I don't understand what you mean at all?"

"In my opinion, the behaviors that you perceive to be sins and transgressions are inherent to human nature. "For example, a sexual relationship is something that everyone needs."

The big sister did not want to talk about these issues and seemed clearly distressed. However, he could not remain silent in front of my comment and said in response:

"Contrary to what you might think, marriage and healthy sexual relationships are not a problem for me." I just don't like promiscuity! But it looks like you are more interested in living this way. "If your family had raised you right, you would have never been drawn to this path."

These mean and dogmatic words made me very infuriated, and I felt more upset than ever. At that moment, it was possible to say or do something that would cause regret later.

If I had lost my temper in that situation and acted inappropriately, I would have been the one who paid the price the most.

The big sister was looking for a good opportunity and an excuse to punish me and rip me off. So I should have been careful and tried not to be trapped into leaving that easily.

I responded to her with the utmost calmness, courtesy, and humility:

84

If I understand you right, you only allow a man and a woman to be close and have a relationship if they are married. If they don't, it's a sin and immorality. "Is that right?"

"Exactly, Do you think otherwise?"

"I am truly sorry, sister, but these types of ideas and beliefs are no longer relevant." "At least, this is the case in today's educated and progressive society."

"So God bless us. If people like you get power in this country, the gates of hell will open to us!"

"Sister, no one believes these statements anymore," I suggest that you leave this area for a bit and engage with the scientific and intellectual community. Perhaps it will alter your way of thinking and...

"I won't argue with you any farther than this, young man. "There is no chance of saving your soul or body since they are so deeply entangled in the muck of corruption and disaster!"

"So let me leave here right now and get lost." It is for the benefit of both of us. Isn't it?"

"As I said before, unfortunately, we cannot give you such permission."

"Why not?! I came here on my own. Furthermore, I did not sign any paperwork or a commitment letter.

"You are right. However, you cannot leave here until you regain your mental and physical health.

We swore in front of God to help people like you! "So you have no choice but to dedicate yourself to this situation."

"You must be kidding me."

"Absolutely not. You are lost and need help finding your way. You are just like a lamb that gets separated from its flock and doesn't know which way to go! Our job is to lead you so that your soul doesn't fall into the hands of demons. So, you have no choice but to stay here and follow these rules for now."

"But you cannot keep me here against my personal will." This violates all ethical and legal standards. "You can be certain that you will face the consequences for this."

The big sister said with a smile:

"Listen to what I'm saying, young man; when you passed through that door, you entered a different world where there are no earthly rules or laws! So, reserve all of your opinions for yourself. "Because they have no regard for this place."

I said very firmly and confidently:

"But this world you rely on will fall apart soon." If you pay close attention, you can hear the roar of those balls that are getting closer and closer to you. I promise that this country will go in a new direction after we win.

"Maybe so. But no force can change what people think and believe about religion. "This world has been like this for hundreds of years."

"Sister, this is not a crusade! It is solely for the advancement of human rights and the development and perfection of this nation. Eventually, as the breeze of enlightenment begins to blow, it will eventually reach here. "Be certain about this."

"So, we have to get ready in every way, or we will lose our faith and beliefs."

"What you call faith is really the same ignorance and superstition that lead people to destruction and evil."

When she heard this, the big sister sprang up and shouted angrily:

"This terrible war has caused such thoughts to grow." You should run to God for protection from people like you."

I also replied in the same tone:

"This nation is making progress toward freedom and democracy. "The very same thing that you and those like you are scared of."

The big sister kept yelling and getting angrier:

"These are all nonsense. Today's youth are only interested in pleasure and debauchery. So that's why you like these so-called progressive ideas."

I didn't want to argue with someone like her. It was clear that I couldn't make her see my point of view and agree with me by using logic and reason.

She was so biased and stuck in her ways of thinking that such a possibility seemed almost impossible and far away.

At the same time, I couldn't stay quiet in the face of all the sanctimonious beliefs and backwardness. I had to stand up for my morals and the values of thousands of other people.

In other words, I was unable to pass indifferently by this massive amount of nonsense and not provide a suitable and honorable response because of my nature, which constantly seeks out the truth and enlightenment. In actuality, I was fulfilling a duty and a spiritual mission.

I should have admitted that, in one instance, she was largely correct. She stated that this is how things have been for centuries.

There's no doubt that political changes don't have much of an effect on how most people feel about religion, and there are always a lot of people who think about these things.

So, you can't hope for a day when none of these beliefs and biases are left behind.

Please don't make snap decisions. I don't have anything against religion or simple believers. Only superstitions and religious biases make me feel this way.

Big sister was one of those people whose very existence, in my opinion, was detrimental to the development and progress of any civilization.

Naturally, everyone has the freedom to think and live the way that they want, as long as they don't go beyond the boundaries of the law, societal norms, and human interactions and force others to live within the confines of their own personal convictions, just like how the big sister and her followers acted.

After a brief pause, I responded to her earlier remarks:

"It seems like you still don't get what democracy and freedom mean. But eventually, you'll realize that no wall can stand in the way of human advancement and enlightenment."

When the big sister heard these comments, she was so angry and hurt that she didn't know what to do and looked confused at me. It appeared as though she had given up the ability to think and speak.

Of course, that didn't really surprise me. She was so caught up in her own power and astonishment that she never imagined that one day, someone would appear in front of her in this manner.

She remained silent for a few seconds while continuing to look at me angrily.

Then, with trembling voice and broken words, she said:

"Get out of my sight soon. I don't want to say anything else to you."

I stood up calmly and stated,

"I'm not interested in continuing this debate either."

I then walked out of there looking pleased. I believed I had won a significant victory, while at the same time, the big sister was writhing in pain and cursing at me in her mind.

I had incited a wave of prejudice and hatred against myself with this behavior, and sooner or later, I would have to deal with the fallout and experience its unpleasant flavor. I did, however, experience an odd sense of satisfaction and relief.

Do you want to know why? Because I was honest and vehemently stood up for my moral convictions and principles

***

When I relayed the account of my encounter with the big sister to the old man, he reacted with such enthusiasm and happiness as if he had been set free from all of his problems and suffering and had been given a new life.

This response fascinated me, and it took me a little bit by surprise as well. He had told me many times before to be careful with what I did and to try not to make the big sister and her people even more upset than this.

But at this moment, he was bursting with joy and excitement to the point of overflowing.

In justifying this behavior, he said:

"When someone has the courage to stand up to forceful words like this, it really makes me happy, even though his behavior is far from careful." I really didn't think you would be so brave and risky. "I wish I could be there and see what she looks like."

"Believe me; I didn't want it to end here." "But she said things that didn't make sense and made me even less likely to believe her."

"What else can you expect this person to do?" I heard that since she was a child, she has lived in churches and monasteries. That is, they put all of this rubbish and nonsense into her head. Anyway, it was time for someone to get out of the way and let her have her turn.

"I agree with you. But it appears that she has had bad dreams about me." "I'm sure she will retaliate just one of these days."

"When one defends the truth, he should expect these things." "But you should not worry too much."

"Why do you say that?"

"You did mention that you are familiar with Colonel Moro, didn't you?" From what I could see, the big sister had a lot of respect for him. Therefore, there is a good chance that she will forgive you as long as you don't annoy her any further than this and don't interfere with the things that she is trying to do.

"I didn't do anything bad or wrong, so now I hope for the grace and forgiveness of others."

"That's right. But you don't have to make her mad any more than this. " "Do you agree?"

"I don't want to do that as long as she chills out and leaves me alone."

"So act like you know what the rules are here." You can only get what you want this way. If you don't, you will fight with each other all the time. "Take this advice from a person who knows more than you do."

"Damn her dad and all of his rules. You expect me to let someone like that crush my pride and sense of self-worth.

"No. That's why I said, "Just pretend."

"Well, what difference does it make?" She doesn't know that I am playing a role. She must be thinking that she has trained me and called the shot.

"She can think whatever she wants to." It's most important to get rid of her as soon as possible. You can write to the colonel and complain if it bothers you too much. Anyway, you are a soldier, which means you have some advantages over people like me."

"You know the colonel well, or you've heard a lot about him?"

"I used to know him for a short time a long time ago. But I haven't met him yet, so I can't say anything."

"You've been here for almost a decade. Why didn't you talk to him? He might be able to help you.

"He's not here very often. I haven't seen him in almost a year or two. Since then, the big sister has forbidden any of us from approaching him.

"For what?"

"I have no idea." They might be hiding something they don't want anyone else to know."

"Do you think they have some secrets?"

"I don't think it is like what you think." But I'm sure she is keeping something from us. "Now, let's skip these words and do something fun."

"Is it even possible to have fun here?!"

"Yes! Even here, there are ways to have fun. Of course, as long as we break a few morals and rules. This doesn't bother you at all."

"I don't know what you're talking about!"

The old man smiled at me in a strange way and said:

"The show will start soon." "I'm sure you've never seen anything like it before."

Then he asked me to lie down very quietly next to him on the ground!

I was surprised and asked:

"For what?"

He was on the ground and said:

"Please believe me." "I'm going to show you something that you won't expect."

"What happens if someone walks in?" "He might have bad and awkward thoughts."

"Do not worry." At this time of the day, no one comes up here. Rest assured about this.

"OK. I just hope you don't pull my leg because I don't feel like joking at all.

"Not at all. There is some news that only I know about."

"Do you mean the downstairs?"

"Yeah"

"How did you find out?"

Very casual. When I was looking for my cigarette stick one day, I saw a small hole in the floor. Here it is. Do you see?

He had a point. There was a hole the size of a finger in the wooden floor of the room. Through this hole, some of the space below could be seen.

I had a pretty good idea of what he was going to show me. But I didn't expect to see something so naked.

Several nuns or young sisters were flirting with each other right under our feet. All of them had taken off their clothes and religious garments and were completely naked.

I have to say that seeing them like this got me excited and a little bit sexually aroused. At the same time, it made me feel guilty because it made me feel ashamed and modest.

I've never been a whimsical or voyeuristic person. But I couldn't stop looking at such a sight. Their actions were seen as a clear violation of the sister's principles and values that surrounded her. Believe me, I looked down at it with a lot of greed and desire because of the same reason. This adventure lasted about an hour until the sisters had enough fun with each other to let out some of their lust.

They really were brave and courageous. If the big sister hears about this, bad and scary things are sure to happen to them.

It was a shame that these pretty girls wasted their lives and youth here. They should have made the most of every moment of their lives instead of being afraid and shaking as they tried to meet their most basic physical and spiritual needs. Things that people think are theirs by nature and cannot be taken away

One of my friends says that if a person has any sense at all, he will never put his feet in places like that.

When I discussed this issue with my smart and experienced friend, he took a stand against me and said:

"You thought they all came here of their own free will."

"Some parents use force or deception to send their children to such institutions in order to eliminate another mouth to feed." They appear to be sacrificing an animal. On the other hand, there are also some people who send their children to such places due to their religious beliefs. Meanwhile, this behavior benefits someone like the big sister the most. "They profit from the ignorance of others and line their own coffers."

"How is it possible?" "Can you explain a little more precisely?"

"Numerous powerful and wealthy individuals in the area are willing to donate their money in this manner." Due to their ignorance, a number of individuals fall into this trap. On the other side, certain individuals seek personal wealth and legitimacy for themselves, especially those who have committed misconduct. There are numerous notable individuals within this group."

"Does the big sister know about this or not?"

"I'm not sure about it. On the other hand, I am ready to wager that she brings in a significant income from this endeavor. Naturally, all of these actions are carried out in the name of assistance, a vow, or a need; hence, they do not have a negative aspect.

"The debts of the poor are sometimes settled with the monastery in a different way."

"For instance, in what way?"

"In whatever way that is possible." If they possess a unique ability that can benefit them in some way, they take advantage of it. "In a nutshell, everybody gets taken advantage of in some way."

"What about you?" "Have you had any special skills that they made use of?"

"Yes, I am a very good carpenter." However, I was not smart enough to hide my ability from them. To sum it up, they abused me as much as possible, just like the pharaohs forced the slaves to do hard and exhausting work.

I confirmed his words and added:

In contrast to the great legacy of the pyramids, which they left behind, these ideas only led to ignorance and destruction.

It goes without saying that not all religious places were run like this at the time, and historical records show that many monasteries and churches did a good job of spreading knowledge and teaching people how to read and write. Monks and nuns were among the few people who could read and write in the Middle Ages. It is safe to say that many of the books written during that time were written by them. All the books in the Middle Ages were written and drawn by hand. Nearly all of the monasteries had libraries and bookhouses where monks studied, transcribed, and wrote books about medicine, history, and philosophy.

Over time, these actions left a useful and valuable mark and led to the thoughts and actions of people with different ideas and more forward-thinking attitudes among the clergy. For example, people like Luther wanted to make big changes to how religion worked and how people thought about it.

Along with the Renaissance and the start of the Age of Enlightenment, these changes kept happening. But they couldn't close the gap and resolve the deep paradox between religion, science, and modernity as much as they wanted to.

Even now, we are more or less dealing with a similar problem, with the main difference being that religion's power has been severely limited, and its guardians have been told they can't directly interfere in personal and political matters.

Of course, we still have a long way to go before we can get rid of all these rules and biases. (An event that might not happen at all.)

Let's skip this topic.

In the course of this conversation, I said a few things that upset my friend a little.

I was under the impression that he had left this group as I had and that he had no religious impulses or proclivities. But in contrast to what I had anticipated, there were veins of faith in these tenets and convictions buried deep inside his nature, which unexpectedly exploded and shocked me a little.

He responded to me after a little argument in a slightly irate tone:

"You are exaggerating, my friend." "I agree that religion has a lot of superstitions mixed in with it, but in some ways, it has led to great things."

"How?"

"I'm talking about the building of all these huge, beautiful churches and other buildings that will blow your mind." Then how can you claim it didn't leave anything behind?

"Friend, this is not a good reason." First and foremost, you should understand that human rights and values are more important than any material possession. "All of these accomplishments are the result of creative and brilliant minds, not the religion of the person."

"If you ask me, they do these things mostly to get people's attention and spread religious ideas."

The old man frowned and said:

"We can't think of all of this as religious hypocrisy." This is not fair at all.

I did not want to keep talking about this. If we kept doing what we were doing, there was a chance that we would get into a fight, and our relationship would get cold.

Therefore, I immediately changed the subject and addressed a different topic.

He understood my aim. Nonetheless, he exhibited no reaction and easily passed it.

We were both in desperate need of friendship and connection with one another, and neither of us wanted to do anything that would make the other uncomfortable.

This did not necessitate that we refrain from openly expressing our ideas and always err on the side of prudence. Only in a few instances did we exercise greater caution and contemplation so as not to jeopardize our friendship and relationship. In fact, it was viewed as a compromise and as benign conservatism, neither of which I found very appealing. However, in that circumstance, it would be advantageous for both of us.

In order to get rid of his discomfort and divert his attention to something else, I jokingly asked:

"Please tell me the truth. Have you ever slept with any of these nuns or not?"

He was a little embarrassed and distressed. It was as if it were the first time that someone talked to him about these issues!

He answered me:

"To tell you the truth, I thought about it a lot." But so far, there has not been a suitable situation.

"Are you kidding me?" Do you not see how incredibly seductive and hot these girls are? They are looking for happiness in any way they can find it. It was sufficient to exert a little bit more effort in order to very simply achieve your goals.

He smiled bitterly and said:

I'm old enough now that I do not have any regrets regarding these things. You should also try not to think about it.

I didn't want to hurt those poor girls in any way, even more, as I was sick and in that suffering condition.

However, I asked:

"Why shouldn't I give it a try?"

The old man said in a warning tone:

"Because if it happens, you put yourself in bad trouble." You don't know what the big sister does to those poor girls.

"Damn the big sister! It's as always as if she should have control over everything we do."

He giggled at me and said:

"It is precise, as you said, and I know it will make you upset."

"Why don't I date her first, then?" She won't be as harsh on us if I can arouse her lust and have a sexual encounter with her. Do not doubt this."

"What an absurd and erroneous notion!"

"You're saying I'm not capable of handling it."

"No. You simply choose the incorrect side. As soon as someone touches that woman, she will be crucified, especially by someone who is seen as being an atheist like you.

"You old man, how simple you are. That bastard nun simply lacks sunshine to make hay. "I'm willing to wager with you on this case."

"Please just keep quiet. We both run the risk of getting into trouble if they hear us." "You don't want to deprive us of these little pleasures."

"You refer to it as pleasure!" "Oh my God, in my opinion, it is nothing more than self-torture."

"You are still very inexperienced and youthful. If not, you would recognize the influence of bias and ignorance. Please try to just listen to this old man's advice and put an end to these ideas and fancies. "Now, let me return to my personal work." You consider and think about what I said very well. OK?"

After saying this, the old man left the room. My anxieties and worries grew with each conversation I had with him, and I was always thinking about new things.

I knew in the depths of my heart that he had every reason to worry. I could not, however, compromise my viewpoint and succumb to all of these dogmatic and medieval laws.

This kind of behavior was ingrained in my personality, and it was difficult to control.

Chapter Three: Another Day

I was lethargic and exhausted that day and did not want to get out of bed. Fortunately, it was not necessary.

The most significant reason that prompted the patients and staff to awaken from their peaceful morning slumber was to join in morning prayers.

Even if stones and fiery lava fell from the sky, the big sister and her followers would not abandon this ceremony and its superstitions.

I considered it a great blessing that their curse prevented me from participating in this ceremony. I was aware, however, that it came at the expense of conflict with these bigoted and superstitious people.

They looked at me with the eyes of an evil and demonic creature who stepped into their safe and sacred space and polluted it.

Of course, every one of them had the motivation to treat me unfairly. So I had to be careful not to give them an excuse.

However, I doubted that I would excel in this sector! Because I was not the kind of guy who would give up in front of forceful and unreasonable remarks and put on the clothing of presence and hypocrisy,

Let's skip over this one. That morning, I discovered something that both shocked and concerned me.

They used to hold prayers in a hall adjoining the main building. According to what I've heard, this location was once utilized as a stable. But, through time, it was transformed into the principal site of prayer.

I had a look inside this property the other day and observed several worrying defects in its corners. The major issue that drew my attention was the extreme dampness of the walls and the main column. There was also a very large crack in the roof.

I had a terrible fear that something horrible was going to take place at that place at any second, causing some individuals to be saddened by it. Concerning this matter, I gave one of the big sisters a warning. However, she did not appear to give my statements any consideration. Evidently, matters of this nature did not rank very high on the priority list of the big sister or her followers.

I had previously met a good number of zealots who held the belief that the torment we experience in this life is similar to a doorway that leads us to salvation in the hereafter. These types of individuals do not place a high priority on the happiness and well-being of themselves and others in the social and material worlds, and they view such pursuits as the root cause of vice and sloth.

Some people even look forward to disasters of any kind and size happening to people. They explain their behavior by saying that disasters are God's punishment for our wrongdoing and the punishment we deserve.

This kind of thinking is not only ludicrous but also exceedingly stupid, and absolutely nothing positive or helpful will result from it. This is something that any intelligent and perceptive person knows. In fact, it was these thoughts and beliefs that ensnared man at the bottom of the well of ignorance and superstition for millennia, preventing him from making progress and excelling in his endeavors.

Seeing such things tremendously distressed me, and it caused a deep wound in both my heart and my soul. In the same breath, it left me feeling disheartened and disillusioned, and it instilled in me a healthy amount of trepidation for the future of my nation. I never imagined that It had been a long time since the industrial revolution, and everything was modernizing and prospering, from science and scientific and creative technologies to philosophy, law, and politics. I found myself caught in this peculiar and oppressive predicament at a time when these things were happening. In a nutshell, all that was necessary to bring humanity to new horizons was made ready.

Even people's perspectives and convictions with regard to their religious practices had undergone profound and encouraging shifts, the most evident manifestation of which was the distancing of religion and politics from one another. However, it seems as though this section of the planet is dancing to the beat set by someone else.

To be honest, all I hoped for was that the ignorance and bigotry that run this place would remain confined to its borders and not make their way to other parts of the free world. If this were to occur, the results would be far more disastrous and horrific than the Black Plague.

After eating breakfast, albeit reluctantly and out of necessity, I climbed back into bed and prepared for a restful and sweet slumber.

I kept turning from side to side and trying to dream and go back to that nice world for an hour. But no matter how hard I tried, I just couldn't get to sleep.

So I wouldn't get bored, I started reading and looking over the religious books and papers that were piled on top of the closet in my room.

Even though it was not at all one of my preferred activities, and even though it was regarded as a form of mental agony, it was not in any way useless.

Over time, I came to realize that to really understand any kind of intellectual attitude; you have to dig deep into its beliefs and written history and look closely at all of its nuances and details. This is the only way to understand their strengths and weaknesses and learn more about the games that religious and political guardians and claimants play.

Before getting into a discussion or debate, one of my teachers always told me to do research and investigate it. Even if you think you know the truth and have proof to back it up.

I've always kept this wise advice in mind and tried not to judge people and their way of life too quickly or before I knew enough about them.

But sometimes, I met people who were the perfect combination of ignorant and humble. In other words, their actions and behavior were so bad and unacceptable that I couldn't tolerate them and had to take a stand against them. Just like the big sister and her followers, each of them was more backward and less smart than the other.

Let's skip this issue.

I kept my mind busy for a couple of hours by reading and doing research, which was very satisfying.

When it was getting close to midday, I began to entertain the idea of leaving the dim crypt and going on a tour of the monastery instead.

However, before I could do anything, I needed to acquire permission from the big sister. They positioned a guard in front of the door, locked it, and proceeded to secure the chamber. It appeared as though felons and other potentially violent individuals were held at that location. To finally receive clearance to exit the room took me close to an hour of my time. It goes without saying that none of us had permission to enter any area outside the monastery's bounds.

We would receive heavy sanctions if we did it. Besides, the location's features and coordinates made escape extremely challenging, if not completely impossible.

The monastery's southern portion looked out over a vast chasm with a terrifyingly steep fall.

I was cautioned not to go close to the edge of this chasm on the first day of my stay. There had apparently been a number of unpleasant and unfortunate events.

They did not, however, erect a fence or other form of security in front of this terrible valley!

I made a small act of foolishness and walked up to the valley's edge. To be completely honest, I was curious as to whether or not it was conceivable to leave in this manner or whether it was truly impossible.

I only needed to glance down to see the valley's depth and steep slope before realizing that this would be like a suicide. But there were other obstacles standing in our way of freedom as well.

There were vast and towering mountain ranges that surrounded the entire area on both sides of this valley. These mountains were nearly hard to traverse. Only experts could complete this. Of course, provided that the atmospheric and meteorological circumstances are perfect.

In reality, there was only one painless and secure entrance and exit from the monastery.

It wouldn't be so difficult to move forward if I could just get over that iron fence. As far as I knew, the main gate was only ever opened when absolutely required.

You must keep in mind how tough it was for me to secure authorization to enter that location. Leaving there was considerably more tough. Particularly for those like us who weren't members of the clergy or the majority of the monastery's workforce.

To suggest that we were just like prisoners there is not an exaggeration.

Therefore, a person who fantasizes about leaving a place will eventually figure out how to deal with challenging circumstances. If things kept going the way they were, I would eventually have to find a way to cross this barrier and go back to the same world I had fled. That world was engulfed in flames and blood at this point. But despite that, I wasn't too bothered by it.

I wish that I had such tremendous strength and might that I could immediately unlock the iron doors of the monastery and go away from this chilly and depressing environment with the other people. If death were to come upon us while we were traveling this path, it would be best for us to seal our spirit and soul away in a crypt like this one.

While I was thinking about these things, I became aware of the nuns' voices as they said the midday prayer and asked God to forgive them.

They begged and pleaded with such sincerity that they were sure they must have done the biggest and worst sins.

I also heard the wailing and writhing of someone who seemed to be torturing or hurting himself in some way.

Things were going on beyond those walls that were horrendous and dreadful, and they made a complete mockery of human reason and logic. If I were to tell my enlightened friends that I have seen such things happen, it is highly possible that they would not take what I said seriously and instead regard it as a joke. The majority of them were of the opinion that the time for such expressions had long since gone and that no one possessed the intestinal fortitude to create and put into practice such laws and customs. I was already aware that some religious groups and practices engage in such superstitious and radical rituals, but I never dreamed that one day I would find myself in a precarious situation somewhere in the world. It was the same as if I had been convicted of a crime and had to perform community service. On the other hand, I did not give this matter a lot of attention and instead focused my attention on the majesty and beauty of nature, which was a stark contrast to the ignorance and prejudice that were contained in this location.

Since I was a kid, I've loved going on trips and seeing sights in the middle of nature.

My father once told me, "You have a free and brave spirit that can't be kept in one place." Just like a rebellious wind that blows in all directions and goes to every thorn hole. If I wanted to tell you about all the fun things I did as a child and teen, it would take hours and make you bored. I just wanted you to know that I loved nature and animals very much.

Even when the battle and war were at their worst, I didn't forget what I cared about and what I was interested in, and whenever I could, I left the camp.

I used to move around to feel better. Of course, I got into trouble and was punished for it more than once.

While I was in this mood and atmosphere, someone came up behind me and threw a warm woolen top over my thin, cold shoulders.

When I turned around, I saw my one and only real friend and companion. The old man was very nice to me and treated me like his own child.

I thanked him warmly and sincerely and then asked"

"Do you know where this strange sound is coming from? It's like someone is being tortured by being tied to four nails."

He laughed and said:

"You are hearing the voice of one of the brothers who is torturing himself right now. I think you know the motivation behind their actions."

"Yes, I am fully aware of their motivations behind doing what they do. But why is he complaining like this so much? It would appear that he lacks the capacity to take pain in stride."

The old man gave the area a thorough examination to ensure that no one else was around.

Then, with much deliberation and caution, he stated:

"If you ask me, all of these things are completely ridiculous. Who in their right mind would do something like that to themselves?"

I continued:

"You're totally right. But you shouldn't think that such people will act in a sensible way. As the saying goes, 'red flowers don't grow in muddy places.'

"You're making a lot of things up. Not every religious person is so superstitious and prejudiced. Even most religious people don't agree with these things."

"I never said anything like that. But based on my own experiences, I realized that religion and extremism could not be completely separated. Such beliefs are also prevalent in popular culture."

"Nicholas, things have changed a lot since then. Don't think that every place will be like this medieval crypt."

"I agree with you. But it only takes a moment of carelessness for this crypt to come out of its cocoon and destroy the world.

"So, you don't follow any religion or set of beliefs?"

"In my opinion, religion is seen as a personal choice that can be respected, but only if it stays within its bounds and it does not impede the way to enlightenment."

"I think you're right. But you are asking what religion is all about. Is it right?"

"Now that you've asked, I'll tell you the truth. My friend, I think this water is poisoned and dirty from the source."

"What do you mean?"

"I think I got my point across very well."

"You are making a mistake. I don't think that religion itself is the problem. It is their fault that they interpret and talk about religion in the wrong way."

"Only you can be fooled by these words. Why don't you finally face the truth?"

"What gives you so much confidence? Do you know yourself as a smarty-pants?"

"I did not say anything like that. If I say something, it's because I like you and want to help you. So don't get mad at me, please."

"OK, forget it. There are enough problems around here to keep us busy. We don't have to argue with each other anymore about these things."

"Yes, you're right. Instead of saying these words, it is better to think about those poor people who were stuck in that crypt. Every time I think about them, my heart hurts."

"They have reached the end of the danger, my friend."

"That is right; however, they should not be in such a dreadful and unfortunate condition."

"What you say is acceptable to me. But no one can achieve anything extraordinary. May God bless us."

"If your only hope is in Him, you will be here for ages, definitely."

"You still have no idea where you have come to; otherwise, you would not have uttered these things."

"Contrary to what you would believe, I am very aware of what is occurring. However, I have no plans to cope with this doddering monk who behaves monastically. After that, both of us will sooner or later wind up in the same spot like those wretched folks. As a result, you shouldn't be passive and disinterested."

"What you say is acceptable to me. But the issue is that we aren't only dealing with the big sister. People around here are very interested in her and have positive things to say about her. It is just for her to say the word, and everyone will go out of their way to help her."

"You've said that before."

"I understand; however, it appears that you did not take my remarks seriously."

"That is not the case. My first experience of interaction with her was enough to convince me that I was dealing with a monster."

"So why do you fight and argue with her so much? You should know better; it's pointless. It's like beating the wind."

"Because I can't help listening to harsh and illogical language. Actually, I'm used to it and have no control over it.

"You must follow her orders as long as you are here, however."

"Thus, we are going to clash and argue with one another all the time."

"You won't emerge from this field as a victor, either. I bet you."

"You seriously underestimated me, old man. You would trust me more if you knew where I was and what I was up to."

"Young man, don't misjudge me. I have no doubt that you are a brave person since you wouldn't have enlisted in this battle if you weren't, but this isn't enough on its own."

"Many people look at your competitor as if she were a saint. When something looks holy, it can't be changed or broken so easily."

"So we have to wait and do nothing while she does whatever she wants. Was that what you had in mind?"

"If you ask me, the only thing we can do is enjoy the rest of our lives to the fullest. Things are different for you, of course. If you can stay here until spring, you will probably get out of here on your own feet."

"I'm not just thinking about myself, though."

"Believe me; I really like your manners. But there is one thing that I find really strange. Didn't you say that you know the colonel and that you have been friends for years? I wonder why he sent you to a place like here."

"I'm not sure. I guess he has no idea what is going on at all."

"If you hear it from me, he knows more about what's going on here than anyone else."

"I really don't know what to say to you. I have to talk to him in person and ask him."

"I don't think you'll have a chance like that any time soon.

"What's your problem with the colonel? Do you dislike him or hold something against him?"

"Before I answer you, can you tell me how your relationship has been lately?"

"I don't understand what you mean?"

"I am curious about how you two got acquainted. Did you meet by chance, or have you known each other in the past?"

"My father counted the colonel among his longtime circle of friends. Since he was a young man, he never missed a chance to visit us at our home."

"That means you had a very close relationship."

"Yes, we did. I can say without hesitation that he treated me just like one of his own children. However, this enjoyable time did not continue for very long."

"How?"

"Their relationship started to go downhill after they had fundamental ideological and political differences. They even came into conflict!"

"Are you kidding me?"

"At the time, my father was a fervent advocate for slavery. They used to argue a lot because of this."

"What did you do in the interim? I mean, which side did you support?"

"I made an effort to stay out of their arguments. Naturally, I largely agreed with the colonel's viewpoints. But I was

108

unable to talk against my father's wishes and support the colonel."

"What kind of person is the colonel? I have heard that he doesn't have an interesting personality."

"In what aspect of personality?"

"They say he is very harsh and strict."

"You heard correctly. He is not particularly forgiving or tolerant of his subordinates. He may be quite tough in enforcing rules and directives at times."

"So, how did you get along with him?"

"To be honest, we had countless disagreements with each other. It got to the point where I wasn't obeying his commands. As a result, I was chastised multiple times."

"So there's a chance he brought you here on purpose."

"I did not get what you meant!"

"Maybe he wanted to kill two birds with one stone. In this way, he will get rid of your troubles and take his revenge on your father."

"I don't think so. We are both on the same front. It's true that we had different ideas in some cases, but not so much that we're still mad at each other. After all, my dad died a long time before I came here."

"Then why did he cause you such trouble?"

"You should not be so pessimistic. As I said earlier, he might not be aware of how bad and miserable things are here."

"You really are a young man with a pure heart. If not, you wouldn't have put so much trust in him."

"How do you know you're so sure?"

"Since I myself sent him a letter and explained everything."

"First, tell me how you managed to give him the letter. You said that you never talked to him closely."

"I gave the letter to one of his subordinates, whom we already knew. He answered me very quickly.

"You're right! Well, what did he say?"

"He gave me a very brief answer and wrote: Everything the big sister does is for your own good. Instead of engaging in idle chatter, you should give your full attention to the monastic life. Perhaps by doing so, both your physical body and your spiritual self will be purified from the pollution."

"It is very strange and unbelievable. There is no way for the colonel to be a religious and strict person."

"I thought so at first until I received his message. Then I realized whom I was attempting to contact."

"So because of this, you have a grudge against him."

"My good friend, this has nothing to do with holding a grudge. If we hadn't come all the way here, I probably wouldn't have brought up this memory at all. I only want to broaden your perspective a little bit."

"Let's skip these words. Do you still have that letter with you or not?"

"Of course. Don't think that I got all this out of my head or that I am exaggerating."

"If what you said is true, maybe we can file a complaint against him."

"Do you mean in a military court?"

"Of course. This letter can be a very important document."

"Is it easy to understand what you are trying to say?! He is a very significant and powerful figure in the country. I seriously doubt that anyone will give any consideration to what we may say. They may even assert that the letter in question is forged. When that time comes, we will be in utter despair. You did not give this any thought at all. Did you?"

Didn't he stamp or sign the paper?

"He only signed it. After all, none of us has anything to gain by pursuing this issue. Especially for you, who are still under his command, it is useless.

"You are right. But..."

"Forget it for now. If you are in a good mood, I want to introduce you to someone else."

"Why not? Do we have any other important things to do?

"God bless you, young man. That poor man is very sick.

"Probably, one of these days, he will end up in the corridor of death. Let's go to see him and console him."

"That is a good idea. But why don't they let him stay in his own room? Keeping him here may hurt him more."

"Now I'll explain why. The big sister always talks about death and the end of the world. They have rituals and ceremonies down there, which have a big effect on the common and uneducated people and make them rely more on their own thoughts and beliefs than they did before. In fact, she takes advantage of their lack of knowledge and ignorance.

"So none of those poor people have infectious diseases."

"No, they tell this lie to keep people from going there to look around. "You are the only one brave enough to do this."

"Of course, you didn't want to know what was going on at that time. I hope you won't spend more time on this than you have to. If you do, you'll put all of us in trouble."

"I really did not think you would tell me this. We shouldn't ignore it because the same bad thing could happen to us one day."

"Oh, my friend, don't say it! I haven't gone a day without thinking about those poor people. Believe me."

"If that is the case, then why do you put up with the big sister for so long? You must choose one of the options. If you are concerned about running into her, please let me know right away so we can end this conversation."

"It seems as though you are not paying attention to the words that I am saying. She is not an ordinary person that we are dealing with here. Someone who views the world from a different perspective is standing in front of you right now. In this person's opinion, people like you are atheists and unbelievers. Therefore, she is free to do whatever she wants with you. You got incredibly lucky by becoming a soldier.

The most important thing is that someone like Colonel Morrow has guaranteed you. If not, it is not clear what has happened to you so far."

"Damn them both." I am approaching death quickly. So I don't have much to lose."

"Don't say that, my friend. Maybe it will end at the cost of losing your pride."

"I am very sorry. Does that mean you feel pride and self-esteem in this situation?"

"Of course not; no sane person wants to be caught in this situation. Believe me; I mean this from the bottom of my heart."

"Then why are you so afraid?"

"Because I don't want the situation to get worse than it is. "Besides, it is possible that others will get into trouble because of your actions."

"Thus, I should not expect any help and support from you and others."

"Please don't get it wrong. As for me, I will do what I can to make things a little better. But we need to take things slowly and with a plan. If you don't do it, it will lead to very bad things. "So bad that you wish you hadn't come here at all."

"What do you expect me to do?"

"All I ask is that you approach potential harm with discretion and an open mind. Therefore, pay attention to the advice of this knowledgeable individual and refrain from making excuses for him. You can be confident that we are capable of doing more beneficial things with some patience and thought."

The old man was right to be so worried. In order to ease his mind, I put a brotherly hand on his shoulder and, with a calm and reassuring tone, told him:

"You are quite correct, my friend. I believe I went a little too far with it. I assure you that from this point forward, I will concentrate more. Are you content now?"

He smiled and said:

"That's it. Now, if you agree, let's go to my room and take some drinks. Then we will go to see my sick friend. What do you say?

I said enthusiastically:

"That is great."

Then we returned to the monastery happily. Meanwhile, we met the big sister, who was talking to one of the nuns.

As soon as she saw me, she frowned and turned away from us as if an incarnated devil had appeared in front of her.

I did not pay any attention to her. Just unlike the old man who went to her quickly and respected her. He flattered her a bit in order to get her permission to see the sick man.

When he came back, I scolded him for his behavior, and then I went to my room sadly.

He also followed me and told me the same words as before in order to justify all his fear and consideration. I had promised him that I would be careful and avoid struggling with the big sister as much as possible. But now, I found that it was not as easy to adapt to such a situation as I had imagined.

We discussed this again for a quarter of an hour and, at the same time, drank some wine. Then we went to see the sick man, who apparently was not far from death.

When I saw him, I was so affected and upset that I forgot all my physical pains and mental worries for a moment. I really did not expect to see someone so young and, at the same time, suffering and sick in front of me.

He was so thin and frail that I couldn't describe him with anything other than skin and bones.

I wondered if all this weakness and extreme thinness were due to his illness or if it was the result of malnutrition and bad and inadequate care that each of us was affected by in some way, and we were struggling with its consequences from the morning till night.

He was suffering from a high fever and chills and was completely delirious, even while he was sleeping. It was abundantly clear that this was not the appropriate time to pay him a visit.

We were just about to leave the room when he opened his eyes and looked at us with fear in his eyes. I had only seen those kinds of looks during the war on the scared faces of those who knew death was just a step away.

When I looked into the depth of his eyes at that time, I did not see any indication of the ardor and vibrancy of life that I had been expecting to see there. It looked like a dead man was getting up from the grave.

But very soon, he came out of this state and showed us a sweet and friendly smile.

Then, with a joy that made us both feel very moved, he said:

"You have no idea what a pleasant dream I had. For the first time in a long time, I had such a dream."

We were both a little surprised to hear this, and we gave each other serious looks. He was delirious and had a fever and chills just a few minutes ago. So, he was like someone who was having a bad and scary dream, not a nice and sweet one.

In any case, we were glad that he got out of that situation and started to feel better.

The old man sat on the edge of the bed next to him, and as he caressed him like a child, he said:

"I am very happy to see you smiling again. Now tell me what dream you had that made you so happy."

The sick young man gave me a special look and said:

"First, introduce your friend to me. Then we will talk about my dream.

I took a step forward and told him my name and my military rank very simply and briefly as if I were introducing myself to the superior officer!

The old man laughed at my expression and said:

"Don't worry, Nicholas. This is not a war camp. Please be a little more comfortable."

I said with an embarrassed expression:

"You are right. Sometimes I forget that I left there. Anyway, nice to meet you, young man."

"Nice to meet you too. You can't imagine how pleased I am to see you. Please come a little further so I can see you better."

To be honest, I was a little distressed at that time.

I had never experienced anything quite like the peculiar and unusual manner in which that young man regarded me before. It appeared as though a highly significant person had paid him a visit at that moment. When he told us about his dream, I finally understood why he was looking at me in such a strange way.

Perhaps, when viewed from your perspective, it seems weird and even a little bit silly. However, he regarded me as a rescuer and believed that my existence at that location was due to something more than the fact that I was sick and physically weak. In fact, he regarded me as a message sent by an authoritative and heavenly power. Someone who is capable of altering everything there and providing a fresh spirit to the body of this icy and cruel environment. I feel obligated to say that, in my judgment, these remarks did not possess even the slightest amount of value or significance and that they were merely the usual superstition of a community. On the other hand, I did not utter a single word to contradict it.

It was really not fair to engage him in conversation about this topic in order to pry the tiniest embers of hope from the depths of his deteriorating being. However, I did so anyway.

It was the least that I could do for such a sick and suffering individual.

He was very happy to see us, talked about everything, and opened his heart to us.

This went on for nearly half an hour until he became ill again. The horrific face of his condition was then revealed in a more naked manner.

He puked up everything he had eaten. He then began shaking and defecating uncontrollably.

We called the nuns and asked for help several times. Nobody came to help us, though. In the end, we all pitched in and did everything we could to help him.

First, we changed his dirty clothes. Then, we used a soft, wet cloth to clean him from head to toe and get rid of the dirt. Finally, we made his bed and put his sheets on it.

The poor young man felt a little bad about what he had done and kept saying sorry to us.

I have been in a similar situation before. So I knew very well what he was going through.

Because of this experience, I was able to help him feel better and get these troubling thoughts out of his head.

All of these tasks were required to be completed by the nuns, sisters, and other servants who lived and worked in the monastery. They made a promise that they would spend their whole lives helping people who were sick or in need.

However, it appeared that they were unconcerned about the unfortunate situation of this young man and the other patients who resided there. Everyone included me grew feebler and more helpless by the day. In my opinion, they purposefully abandoned this poor and blameless young man so that the specter of death could gradually encircle him, and then they could finally get rid of him. They only did some of his work because they felt they had no choice but to comply with his demands.

I know that these words seem a bit harsh and cruel in the eyes of religious people and believers and will probably offend them.

It is important to bear in mind, however, that the behavior and interactions of members of this congregation with other people were the primary factors that led me to reach this conclusion and not the religion or beliefs that they had in their hearts.

They spent the majority of their time praying and participating in religious rituals, and as a result, they became increasingly removed from the realities of everyday life.

They didn't even bat an eye when asked to offer these vulnerable people a simple smile or a word of encouragement in an effort to alleviate some of the anguish and suffering that was brought on by the disease.

By the way, when we tried to leave him, he hardly shook himself and instead pointed his finger toward the window.

At first, we believed that he was trying to invite more natural light and air into the space. But we were completely incorrect.

While we were doing this, he requested that we bring him close to the window ledge so that he could look outside. A few minutes were needed to carry his frail and helpless body to the window.

He had gotten so weak and fragile that a simple, sudden movement could make him angry and upset.

While we were watching him from behind, he put his head out of the window and took a deep breath of the fresh air. It seemed like he had been waiting for this moment for a long time.

At that time, it was a bit cold and cloudy, and we were worried that it would make his condition worse, but it didn't seem to bother him.

While he was in this state, he looked around with curiosity and excitement and said:

"I heard you made a snowman. Can I see it from here?"

None of us anticipated that he would pursue it with such fervor.

It turned out that the action, which we had thought was stupid and childish and just ignored, had given this place unique and unexpected energy and brightened some of its dark and cold corners.

Who knows, maybe this action might represent the big sister's battle and revolt, freeing her from the thorn of authority. But it was unfortunate because there was no sign of that snowman.

As soon as we left, I vowed to do everything in my power to help the young guy before his sickness and weakness overtook him completely and brought him to his knees.

He hadn't slept with a woman yet, as others had said. If we could give him this chance, it would make him feel better.

We were sorry, but the situation did not make it easy for us to do this for him. After that, he no longer had the strength to do these things.

In any case, we were both tired of this situation and wanted to do something useful and positive. But we didn't know how to get out of this terrible situation.

Chapter Four: Funeral

I was eating breakfast when the old man with a sad face came into my room and told me that the young man had died.

I wasn't surprised by this news, to be honest. We both thought that would happen. But we didn't think we'd have to say goodbye to that nice young man so soon.

We were talking about what was happening when one of the nuns walked in. She told us both very harshly and firmly to get ready for the funeral service.

I funnily talked to him and told her:

"You didn't need to give orders." "We were also getting ready."

She was angry with my words and said:

"You can't do it with this outward appearance and clothes!" You have to get ready in any way. If not, you don't deserve to attend this event.

Then, while she was muttering and whispering curse words, she left the room.

I cursed behind her as well and blew off steam somehow.

A few minutes later, another sister came in and gave me a dark, rough dress that I had to wear to the ceremony.

Everyone who lived in the monastery, no matter how big or small, had to take part in this ceremony, and no excuse was acceptable.

Those who did not follow this order would be severely punished. In this case, there was no kindness, and the people who didn't do what they were told were treated harshly and brutally!

Of course, this ceremony wasn't held that simply, and it had its strange rituals.

I didn't want the big sister and the people around her to treat me like a puppet.

But in this situation, it wouldn't be smart for me to play the Devil's Advocate and make this hard-hearted and bigoted group even angrier at me. So, without any ifs or buts, I agreed to take part in this ceremony.

My friend was a little surprised by my choice. He thought I would behave more obstinately and stubbornly, which was neither strange nor unexpected. He thought that way because of what I had done and how I had acted. But he seemed to be happy with my decision.

Contrary to what the old man expected, I had exercised foresight and erred on the side of caution, but don't think I made this change in behavior and procedure lightly.

I'm sure you've figured out so far that I'm not one of those people who can easily change their morals and personalities and act differently. Even when things were at their worst, I tried to stick to my morals and standards as much as possible. and choose the right and most logical thing to do.

At that moment, I felt like I had no choice but to go along with a wrongful and humiliating act.

My rebellious and truth-seeking nature was constantly challenged by the big sister's rules and commands, which went against everything I believed to be right and good. Simply because I cared about my friends and what they were going through, I tried to be accommodating to the big sister and her people.

We joined them as they were praying on the bed of the dead body.

We waited in a corner of the room for half an hour until the big sister came in with her ostentation and told her people to take the body down to the cellar.

We also moved very quietly behind them, while our hearts and minds were millions of miles away from them.

I was happy in one way, of course! The poor young man was lucky that he didn't live much longer than this, and he left the land of nothingness very quickly. If he didn't, he'd be sent to death row. In this case, he would have spent his last hours in a much worse place.

The big sister and her people didn't seem too happy about this. I already told you that this group saw pain and suffering as ways to make the soul shine and get rid of sins, so they welcomed them with open arms.

They had planned to use the death of our loved friend in more ways. So it wasn't a big surprise that they were so angry.

But I knew this group of people well enough to know that they would make the best of the situation.

As we went down the stairs to the cellar, I had a strange feeling of fear and anxiety that made me shiver from head to toe.

I knew what this feeling was like. When I was first sent to the front lines, I had to face the enemy. That day, I had a lot of good luck.

If my other friends hadn't helped and died for me, I might not have lived through much of that death. But I'd rather be in that hard and horrible situation than this miserable and humiliating one. Believe me, I'm telling you this from the bottom of my heart.

When we went a little lower, we found a strange and scary atmosphere that seemed to affect everyone at the ceremony, especially those who had never been there before.

Cone-shaped statues were placed all around the cellar, surrounded by crooked Latin lines.

But a pile of skulls and bones that filled the space between these statues was what people were most attracted to, or rather, what made them feel scared and unsafe.

The bones were put on top of each other very neatly and carefully to make a wall. There were also some torches between them.

I have to confess that the big sister and her followers did a good job setting up this scene.

The place was really scary and hallucinatory. It felt like we had walked into a tomb that was ready to swallow our souls.

We were all affected in some way by this space and the heavy feeling that surrounded it, and we all wondered what was going to happen.

We waited for an hour in terrifying silence until the preparations were made.

When everything was set up according to what the big sister thought and wished, the dead body was completely naked in front of our astonished eyes and placed on a stone slab like a coffin in the middle of the cellar.

Then it was washed and scented carefully and patiently. In the end, they wrapped a white cloth around it, which gave it a mummy-like appearance.

During this whole time, some people, like apostles, prayed as they walked around the body.

Behind them, a group of people was lying on the ground, begging and lamenting very ecstatically.

I was really surprised to see this scene. It was as if I had walked into a tribe that was far from civilization and full of superstitious rituals and monstrous customs.

The big sister was at the top of this pyramid. She was standing alone in a corner and looking at everyone and everything with a cold and angry face. She sometimes told other people what to do and what not to do, just like a powerful master and commander who puts her servants and workers in a circle around her court.

She was interested in this ceremony that was based on superstition, and she used it well to grow her power.

This is true of everyone who thinks religion is a good way to get what they want and achieve their goals and who uses religion to control a large number of people and make the weakest minds stronger.

The big sister was one of these people, but what made him different was that she cared about these things. That is, she wasn't someone who pretended and tried to hide things.

When she saw me, she again scrunched up her face and gave me that ugly, mean-spirited look. The disciples and the people around them also showed a similar reaction.

I didn't want to deal with them any longer.

But the way they acted made me even more skeptical and made me show a reaction.

I left the ceremony in a bad mood, muttering curse words as it was still going on.

It was the first time that someone did something like this during the funeral service. It was seen as a big insult to the big sister and everything she held holy and important.

Naturally, the big sister wasn't too upset about this. The way she looked and the barely perceptible smile on her face gave away this reality.

This was a nice excuse I had given her.

She could now harass me more readily than before, which would make my life more miserable.

It was also possible that she would accuse me of blasphemy and atheism and give me a punishment that was so harsh and horrible that it would hurt like hell.

But it was all over, and it was no use crying over the split milk.

I was going to go back to my room to rest and study for the rest of the day. But they didn't tell me I could do that. So I had to wait in a corner until that superstitious ceremony was over.

I was drowning when a crew member came up to me with digging tools and told me in a very rude and shocking way to follow him.

124

When I asked why he said:

"We have to dig a new grave." I hope you'll be able to do it. "You seem very weak and helpless."

"What's the point?" "Shouldn't you do this?"

"No one here asks questions; they just do what the big sister tells them to do." Understood?"

"I see what you mean." "But I'm not the kind of person you might think I am."

"So you're not willing to help me." "I could guess that you don't have the guts or the grit."

Listen! I grew up on a farm. So I am not afraid of hard work. I just don't like anyone ordering or forbidding me.

"So, how did you join the military?" "Don't you have to do what your superiors tell you to do?"

"Does what you're saying make sense?" You're saying that this crypt is like the army. Shame on you!

"Don't think I'll beg you."

"No. I don't expect you to do anything! "But you can be more kind and respectful to other people."

"I don't feel like arguing with you." If you want to help me, take this pickaxe and come with me. If not, get the hell out of here.

"Ok, I'll come with you, but it's not because the big sister said so." "I just want to show you that I can do this without much trouble."

The man gave me a dirty look and said, "Whatever you say."

Then he spat on the ground where my feet were.

His behavior was very insulting and shocking, like that of the other people who were spiritually affected by the big sister.

Their goal was to hurt my pride and sense of self-worth as much as possible, scare me, and force me to do what they wanted. But they didn't know that my inner resolve to face them was growing stronger by the minute.

***

We worked hard and sweated for almost an hour until the frozen, hard ground finally gave way. During this time, the big sister and her followers came to check on our work several times. They kept an eye on every aspect. From the width and depth of the burial to other, in my opinion, less significant and crucial things.

They regarded this matter with a lot of zeal and enthusiasm. It appeared as though we were producing a priceless work of art.

However, this kind of behavior did not particularly surprise me, as I was aware of the significance and place that pain and death held in these people's views.

As a matter of fact, I knew very well that big sister thoroughly relishes my pain and suffering. That's why she gave me this hard and exhausting work to do. She even asked us to dig the grave a little deeper than usual, which bothered me even more.

When we were done with this job, I was so tired and hurt that I couldn't get out of the grave without help from my friend.

At this time, I noticed that the big sister and her friends had smiles that were both subtle and teasing.

They probably thought to themselves that they had hurt my pride and dealt a hard blow to my stubborn and brave spirit.

This was a crazy and stupid way of thinking that only made their sick minds even worse.

One of the thinkers said that once a person has tasted freedom and truth, they won't be afraid of dogmatists and superstitions and won't be ruled by them.

By the way, I didn't plan to stay there until the ceremony was over. I was tired and didn't want to do anything, on the one hand. On the other hand, it drove me crazy when the big sister talked nonsense. But I changed my mind to honor our late friend.

I observed the features of those in attendance while the funeral was being conducted slowly and passively. Among them, I observed unfamiliar and new people with unremarkable facial expressions. In other words, it would not be obvious that they are here out of dread of the big sister or because they sincerely believe in these false traditions.

One of them was a man in his forties or fifties who wore a long, thick fur coat. However, we were wearing ordinary clothes that weren't very warm, and we were shivering from the cold.

The rules and regulations that the older sister had set up said that no one could come to the monastery with such an outward appearance.

He probably had a lot of power and respect there, which gave him some freedom from these laws. In short, he wasn't the kind of person who would catch my eye and make me want to be with him. After asking a few questions, I realized that we are not only spiritually and morally different, but also have very different ideas and thoughts.

People called him Sergeant Sam Smith.

It was said that he had shown a lot of bravery and selflessness in the war with the Northern Alliance, which, from my point of view, was pure cruelty.

But I couldn't judge it based on rumors or what other people said about it.

Who knows—maybe living in this place affected his mind and thoughts and made him change and grow on the inside. I didn't know this until we spent some time with him and talked together.

If he answered my few questions honestly, I would learn more about his morals and thoughts and get to know him better. It was also possible that all his words and claims were fake and he just meant to show off. Of course, if what other people say about him is true.

During my service, I met a lot of people like him.

When these people are heard, they usually become enraged. They lie and distract from the truth to get people's attention.

To be honest, I have to say that I have sometimes used this method for something else.

Especially when I was drunk and losing touch with reality, or when I wanted to expose the other party's crimes and brutality and arouse the emotions of the others.

This is a kind of rhetorical trick, sophistry, and the fallacy of speech that almost everyone uses to try to impress others and get his way in the end. Even those who aren't naturally liars or hypocrites but try to move in the right and sensible direction sometimes use this trick.

The truth is that this kind of thing happens a lot in every war and intellectual conflict.

Only knowledgeable and meticulous people can distinguish between the pure and absolute truth from lies and illogical or convenient reasons and choose the right path.

You might wonder what will happen to ordinary people with less education in the meantime. How do they tell the difference between the truth and lies and pick the right path?

To answer this question, we should focus on the role of wise and open-minded people.

When it came to the important event I was a part of, there was no question about which side was right. One side wanted to keep slaves and keep doing things the wrong way like in the past, while the other side talked about freedom and equality for all people. Anyone who is smart and can see the future can see that if we fail, it will hurt society and all freedom seekers, and it will lead the country into chaos and instability. I'm not saying that we didn't make any mistakes, though. There were a lot of problems with us that needed to be fixed right away.

If not, our hopes and dreams would be blown away, and the time of darkness would continue.

Now I'll skip this section and tell you about the adventures I had that cold and miserable morning.

Another person who caught my eye was a young and handsome man whose body was coursing by a slight tremor.

I thought at first that he was shaking because it was cold. But after I found out why, I became even more worried and upset.

This poor man had a secret relationship with a nun and slept with her, so he was severely tortured, and because of this, he was suffering so much.

So much mental and physical abuse was done to them that none of them went back to how they were before, and they all lost their emotional and mental balance completely.

No one knew for sure what happened to that nun. After a few days, they told people that she had left the place. No one, of course, thought this was true, except those who had no choice but to believe the big sister and did not question anything she said.

She probably died because she was persecuted a lot and because of the problems that came from that. There was also the chance that she killed herself so she wouldn't have to go through any more pain and humiliation.

In the view of many families, such acts were a source of shame and dishonor, causing them to be shunned in society.

Now I had a better idea of what was going on and why they were so afraid of the big sister and her followers. I have to be honest and say that at that very moment, my resolve to address her more directly was somewhat weakened.

To be more specific, the cloud of worry and uncertainty was slowly casting its shadow over me.

I was struggling with these kinds of thoughts when someone put his hand on my shoulder.

When I turned around, I saw that veteran's friendly face. I'm referring to the guy in the fur coat.

At that time, I didn't want to talk to him.

But, I gave a cordial response to his greeting since I didn't want him to have a negative impression of me.

His actions were good and polite enough to give me hope that our friendship and relationship would last.

I was talking to him when one of the nuns came up to us and asked us to be quiet during the ceremony.

The big sister rolled her eyes at both of us as well.

I wasn't scared by the way she looked, but because I respected my late friend, I did what she asked.

We were all worn out and irritated since the ceremony ran much longer than normal.

When our friend's body was eventually buried without anyone crying for him, it was almost midday.

Only my friends and I showed how sad we were and paid tribute to his memory in public.

This behavior infuriated the big sister, who saw it as disobedience and rebellion. It was as if we were unable to laugh or cry without her permission.

After the ceremony was over, everyone was told to meet in the hall.

My friends and I stayed for a while until we were the only ones there. Other people went back to the fold like a flock of sheep.

Please don't get it wrong. I don't want to insult and humiliate other people. I used this comparison so that you could better understand how this place works.

We were the only ones who didn't obey them completely and tried to ignore as many of their rules and orders as possible.

In this case, we wanted to say goodbye to that dear friend in a way that he deserved and wanted.

This wasn't much to ask. But we were up against someone who thought these kinds of actions were against custom and broke rules. In other words, they thought of it as a kind of sin that needed to be punished!

We didn't care about this situation, and we went on with what we desired to do.

The old man acted as a priest and prayed for the peace of the late young man's soul. In addition, he lauded his virtuous acts and paid tribute to his memory. We also accompany him. After that, we joined the other people who were gathered together to hear the older sister's speech and the repeated sermons that she gave.

She was instructing them, as she often did, on the need to have faith and avoid sin as well as pride. When she looked in our direction, she abruptly changed the subject and began extolling the virtues and moral traits of the young man, and she begged all of us to make him our example. This woman's level of insolence and shamelessness knew no bounds at any point in time.

We were all aware of the fact that she did not give a hoot about these unfortunate people.

It was only when they were about to die that she showed up at their bedside and remained there with an intensity of joy and passion that words cannot adequately describe until the very end. Because of this, some people referred to her as the angel of death.

From what I heard, she never went to see that young man or asked how he was doing while he was in pain and writhing around.

In other words, she didn't know anything about him or his morals.

After she finished her sermon, she told her subordinates to bring us all a cup of coffee and a piece of cake.

I'll never forget the way her face looked at that moment.

She looked at us with such pride and arrogance that you thought she had done us a big favor.

It was as if we were her servants and subjects, and we had no choice but to live under those conditions.

The big sister did everything she could to get people to listen to her and do what she wanted. She influenced the naive people in this way by using a policy of rewards and punishments, or "carrot and stick."

We three were not a part of this group. But whether we like it or not, her medieval ideas and regulations had an impact on us.

When a member of staff blocked my path and requested that I wait there in an extremely rude and insulting manner, I was ready to return to my room.

Nothing was left for me to do that would cause me to lose my patience and tolerance for such behavior and ruin everything. If my friends hadn't stepped in and taken control of the situation, I would have fought with the man.

They put me in a corner and gave me coffee and cake to make me feel better. But I was even angrier than I was before!

I am not and have never been a very picky or hard-to-please person. But I didn't think they would give us such disgusting food that day.

The taste of that cake and coffee, if you can call it that, was so awful that it made us all feel sick.

It seemed like they did it on purpose to make us suffer even more.

We were laughing about this problem when the door to the hall opened and some locals walked in.

They were holding trays that were pretty big and had a lot of small clay dishes on each one.

They put a colorful, glazed potion inside these dishes. It must have tasted good, or else people wouldn't dribble or seem bright-eyed and bushy-tailed about eating it.

Seeing this scene was annoying and made me feel bad about myself.

I, like other people, longed for good, healthy food. I don't want to lie about this. But my pride wouldn't let me put up with such shame. In other words, I didn't want to make the big sister and her people happy by making them laugh at such a sad scene.

This group took every chance to put us down and hurt us. They tried to hurt our pride and sense of self-worth as much as they could. They acted in this manner because they were afraid of the spirit of unity and solidarity that was emerging among us.

I hope to live long enough to see democracy win and the rule of law take hold in this wonderful country. This is the only way to get to the source of liberation and freedom and get rid of these backward ideas.

Please don't get it wrong. I do not want religion to be eliminated from all aspects of social life. That is not the case.

It makes no sense and is not possible. It is only necessary that religion stay far away from law and politics, as well as people's personal and social freedoms, and stay within the four walls of the church and other religious places. If we don't, we'll lose all the progress we've made and slowly fall behind.

The Renaissance and Industrial Revolution helped us make up a little bit for how far behind we were and move more quickly toward progress and enlightenment.

I don't have to tell you how much pain and suffering we had to go through to get to this point so that the fresh breeze of modernity and freedom could blow again and refresh our souls. But we can't forget that the monster of dogmatic views and regression can't be destroyed and erased from the world.

I think that as long as there are people in this world, the demon of ignorance and tyranny will continue to live with them and occasionally flare up. It's important not to give it more chances to show off and defy.

I hope these things didn't make you bored. I have no idea when these pieces of writing will be read. Of course, with the hope that it will not be destroyed by time and that someone will notice it. I only hope that it will give some people new ideas and make them more aware of my life and the changes in American society at a time when they are most important.

By the way, my friends did me a favor by keeping a bowl of that fragrant potion for me.

When I tried it, I understood why other people liked it so much.

I have to say it was one of the best food I've ever eaten. It was so good and delicious that it made me feel better about having to go to this event and took my mind off of it for a while.

Actually, the continuous and pervasive fear had given way to a sweet and fleeting euphoria with the intention of soothing the simple-hearted and creating a false image of the monster's forgiveness and mercy in their minds. This was the traditional and repetitive tale of lust and fear, which is evidently reflected in believers' notions of hell and heaven.

Religious leaders and missionaries have used these beliefs for centuries to seduce and trick believers into doing what they want. They do everything they can to make people think and act in this bigoted and superstitious way.

I was very familiar with these fake and misleading movements, and they had no effect on me at all, which was why they hated me so much.

As I had thought, these dogmatic and unskillful people couldn't have made such delicious food and dessert.

Several hardworking women and girls from the village came here to pay for their vows and needs honestly and sincerely.

They were called here very early in the morning to help the big sister and her disciples.

In such cases, they let the people in the nearby villages know about a special and important ceremony by ringing the bell.

The locals also stopped what they were doing right away and came here quickly. It's as if their god and prophet are calling them!

These uneducated and simple-minded people, who gathered around the big sister like a flock of sheep and followed her lead, looked to her as their shepherd and guide.

They were unaware that they weren't particularly valuable to her.

They served just as a means for her to fulfill her heinous and incredibly reactive wants.

She did not believe that her behavior was wrong. She erred in believing that she is leading us to salvation and has chosen the right and heavenly path. If she didn't, she wouldn't be so demanding of others and wouldn't make their lives so miserable.

I didn't like her or what she thought. I agree that hatred and evil are not traits of freethinkers and that they destroy the human spirit. But sometimes we meet people who try to make us do things that go against our values and beliefs. I've already talked briefly about this problem. In other words, the worst nightmare of a smart, free thinker is to see people like this in charge. In these situations, people show what they are like and what they are made of. People who are weak and don't care about anything crawl into a corner and let anything humiliating or embarrassing happen to them.

They sometimes go with demons to avoid getting hurt by their poisonous stings and venom.

On the other hand, some people care more about the success and growth of society than their comfort and happiness, and they stand up bravely against oppression and unfairness.

Up until that day, the big sister was the most hateful person I had ever met.

She stood in a corner with a proud look on her face and was in charge of all the work without any sign of pity or kindness in the depth of her eyes.

How did she and her followers feel about life?

They were so caught up in their fake and empty world that they didn't notice or care about anyone else. They couldn't even understand people's most basic and obvious needs and desires.

Could she understand the desire to see new places and meet new people? Could she feel the joy of kissing and hugging the people we love?

Now, let's skip hugging and making love with the loved one since it has no place in her mind or imagination.

Could she see the spark of passion and hope for life in the eyes of that simple, hardworking farmer who, after months of suffering, hard work, and fear of natural disasters, finally pulls his bountiful harvest from the ground?

Did she ever wake up one morning and, instead of praying over and over, look up at the sky at dawn because it was so beautiful? It is a time when the morning breeze gets deep into us and fills our souls with real spirituality.

I wish she could feel the pleasant warmth of the soft beach sand under her feet and give her body freely to the sea waves without any covering. I wish she could understand family love and the joy of motherhood as well as she should.

All of these things are part of the world's beauty and wonder, but people like her rarely take advantage of them.

I don't think they've even given it much thought. If they had, they wouldn't have put themselves in that situation.

In these people's minds, the world and everything in it came from that illusory sin that kept people from living in the heavenly house and sent them to suffer in this world instead.

At that time, these kinds of thoughts were so poisonous and illogical that they had no place in religion either.

Such narrow views were only common among fanatics and other extreme groups.

The old man took my hand and led me to a quiet corner of the hall while I was thinking about these things.

Then he whispered in my ear very quietly:

"Two of the sisters are going to run away tonight."

I asked in a tone that was a mix of surprise, happiness, and satisfaction: "Are you sure?"

He nodded and said,

"I heard it."

"Are they those nuns who were together that night and...?"

"That's right. I already knew that they would think about leaving at some point.

"How did you hear about it?"

"When we said goodbye last night, the devil tempted me to take another look at that hole. Then I understood what they were going to do."

"It isn't of the devil or a bad thing to do, my brother. "It is just because of our wants and needs that make us think about these things."

"It is not the right time to talk about these things." We must be vigilant so that we can assist them if they require assistance.

"What should we do?"

"We can give them food and money, as well as anything else that will help them get away." I have a few dollars saved up. "How about you?"

"I think I have about ten dollars in the bottom of my pocket!" But I don't think this is a good plan, though. If you ask me, we need to find a way to stop them.

"Why should we do such a thing?"

"Because this isn't the right time." The best thing to do is to wait until the snow melts. You know better than anyone how hard and dangerous it is to get through that crossing. "It is even harder, especially for two young girls who aren't strong enough."

The old man had a few thoughts and fought with himself. He wanted to help these two people and make it possible for them to get away in any way he could. But in the end, he realized that doing something like that wouldn't help them and would put their lives in danger.

Now, one of us had to step up and tell them how dangerous it was to do this. It wasn't easy.

The first thing we had to do was win their trust.

We couldn't tell those girls where we heard about this. If they found out about the hole in the floor and our peeps, they would think badly of us.

But this wasn't our most important problem. As I said before, none of us were allowed to meet and talk with the nuns without permission, even if they were lower in rank and position.

Due to bias and sensitivity in this field, the nuns also tried to stay away from us as much as possible. If someone broke these rules, she would be severely reprimanded and punished. Some of these punishments included being put in the cellar and even getting beaten. In the worst cases, the person thought to be guilty was burned and marked. This suffering was seen as a sign of his sin and guilt, and it would be with him until the end of his life.

I really could not stand such embarrassment and humiliation. If someone treated me like this, I would do whatever I could to protect my honor and dignity and teach him a lesson.

After talking about it, we decided that it wouldn't be smart to get close to them and talk to them face-to-face because we were afraid that someone would find out and tell about it the big sister.

The best way to warn them was to drop a note through the hole in the floor. But on that night, none of them were there. It was as if they were up to something we didn't know about.

Chapter Five: A New Friend

I awoke very early in the morning to the clamor of the big sister and her people.

She kept calling out,

They got them in trouble. They misled them. Demons, demons... I know they did it. I swear to God!

I knew right away where all this anger and hatred was coming from.

It seems that while we were all sleeping, those girls took the chance and ran away.

On the one hand, this event made me happy and hopeful. On the other hand, it made me anxious and worried.

They probably wouldn't be able to easily get through that impassable crossing and get far enough away from the big sister's territory, unless they got lucky.

I was having the same thoughts and dreams when my friend walked in with a smile and a lot of energy and said,

The birds got out of the cage! You can't imagine how amazing and nice they did it.

Then, in an odd and humorous display of joy, he began to dance as though he, too, had been released from this prison and its invisible chains.

I have to say that those girls did a great job and deserve praise for it. Unfortunately, we didn't have anything to drink at the time. We would have clinked our cups in their honor otherwise. Now we could only wish them well and hope that they survive this danger. After a while, the old man stopped being so happy and excited and instead looked sad and worried. It was like he was no longer drunk and had his wits back.

When I asked him what was wrong, he answered sadly and desperately,

The big sister sent some professionals who know very well what to do. I'm sure the poor girls will be killed if they don't get to the crossing by noon. Certainly, as long as they are still alive.

My friend, it's better to look on the bright side. The girls are several hours ahead of the big sister's people. So there is a good chance that they can make it. Right?

I don't want to sow seeds of despair in your heart and make you feel sad. But you can't avoid the truth.

Which truth are you talking about?

No one has been able to get out of this hellhole so far.

But that's not a good reason, though. Maybe this time they'll get lucky and...

My friend, luck doesn't matter much here. They should be ready for everything and stick to the plan. If not, it will end in disaster. You thought the same at first you heard about it. Didn't you?

You're right. But I have a lot of faith in their success.

I wish I could feel the same way. Throw away these bad ideas and thoughts. I saw those girls, and they are very smart and brave. I'm sure they thought of everything ahead of time. It does not help to be in a bad mood and feel irritated, though. We just need to wait for new news.

Who knows, maybe they made it across the valley safely and are enjoying their freedom right now as we are talking.

I hope it is as you say. But I worry more about the people who live there. No one knows what will happen to them if they get caught by them.

So, you mean something like this happened here in the past?

Quite a few times.

Has anyone been able to get away?

No, I'm afraid not. Last time, one of the girls ran away in the spring of last year. We didn't know about her until they found her naked and half-dead under the waterfall after a few days. It turned out that they had hurt her badly. Do you get what I'm saying?

Of course

The poor girl tried hard to stay alive for a few days before she finally gave up. You have no idea what a good and pure girl she was. I still feel like my daughter is gone. Curse everyone who made this terrible thing happen to him.

How did the big sister behave?

What were you hoping she would do? She got through it quickly and easily, as if nothing had happened. It's not strange, of course. Because here, anyone who goes against her is seen as an atheist and an unbeliever, and he or she can be hurt in any way. In another word, this is regarded as a punishment for her sin. Even if that girl came back and said she was sorry, she would still be punished so that other people would learn from her mistake.

But these girls surely have families. How does she tell their families about it?

It's not a hard thing to do. Most of these girls were left here by families who don't care if they are there or not. Even once a year, they don't hear from them.

The other families are so religious and fanatical that they can't stand this shame. They gave it to the church so that it could decide what to do with their lives.

That's right. But sitting around and doing nothing is not the right strategy.

What do you think we should do?

We have to get out of this hellhole and tell the rest of the world what's going on. We have to do this. Don't you agree?

I know how you feel, but this won't help.

Why do you talk this way?!

Did you think that someone would care about these words in the middle of this war and all this nonsense?

Do you want to just sit there and do nothing? This has nothing to do with honor or morals.

I didn't say anything like that. All we have to do is wait for the right time.

You've lived here for almost a decade. You would have done what you were going to do by now if you were going to do it.

What did you think I would do?

I have no idea. At least you could explain what's going on to a few people. It might have made someone feel something and made them want to do something about it.

You have no right to judge me that way. I tried as hard as I could. You can't even imagine how much pain and anger this caused me.

I'm sorry. I know that I shouldn't have said that. I hope it won't change how we feel about each other.

Oh, take it easy. Best friends sometimes get mad at each other and have arguments over certain matters.

I agree with you. Now let's go see that sergeant I met yesterday if you agree. He might know something that we don't.

But I thought you didn't like him because he used to be in the military and there were rumors about him.

At first, I thought like this. But when I talked to him, his morals and behaviour impressed me. After that, I think it would be best to move closer to each other. Who knows? Maybe we will need his help in the future. From what I've heard, he gets along well with everyone here. So, it's likely that we'll learn more about everything.

OK, do whatever you think is right. But remember that his ideas and thoughts are very different from yours. He might say something that makes you angry.

Don't worry, buddy. I've had relationships with people who are worse than this, but I've never caved into them.

What if he says something insulting and pointless? Do you promise not to get mad and argue with him?

I don't think he's that kind of guy. You most likely made a quick decision about him.

I have known him for four years. So I don't say things I don't understand.

I meant that it might be different now. When was the last time you talked to him?

I don't know him that well. We only talk to each other to say hello!

So you still don't know him.

I understand it well enough to...

If it's okay with you, I'd like to rely on my sense and experience and not on words and rumors.

"Do whatever you want," the old man said in a grumpy tone. Anyway, I already told you what I needed to say. From now on, it's up to you.

I don't know what he meant by saying these words. Was he trying to help me by telling me not to get to know that person better, or was he just jealous and saying bad things about him behind his back?

No matter what the reason was, it didn't make an impression on me. If anything, it made me want to learn more about that man and the deeper meanings of his morals and beliefs.

After an hour

That man smiled at us as he opened the door to his room and led us inside with great pride and honor. It was as if two very important and good people had come to see him.

As soon as I walked in, I could smell the strong smell of tobacco and some kind of drug which tickled my nose a bit. It seems that our friend smoked a little bit. I couldn't believe that he had set up such a feast for himself, away from the big sister and his followers.

At the same time, I noticed the number of medals and combat ranks that were neatly hung on the wall.

He was not in a position or military rank that would have allowed him to win so many medals and military ranks.

My first thought was that he got all of these medals and badges by doing something wrong and dishonorable. But I couldn't judge or come to any conclusions based on this.

I should have talked to him about this issue when the time was right, and then I would have known a little more about his work. Maybe the truth wasn't what it seemed to be at first glance.

He greeted us warmly and sincerely. Then he put us at a table in the corner of the room and gave us services politely and courteously.

Even though we were very different in personality and military experience, I couldn't hide the fact that he was a very nice and welcoming person. I couldn't help but praise him when I spoke.

The old man was not happy with how things were going, and he let everyone know about it. He probably thought to himself, "Now I won't take what he says about how people act and who they are too serious."

But it seemed too soon to decide this. Who knew? Maybe a very scary and strange monster was sleeping behind all the unexpected warmth and closeness he showed. Just passing time could somehow show us his real personality and face.

You might wonder why I say "somehow." The answer is easy to figure out. The truth is that you can't find out all of a person's secrets, personality traits, inner interests, and attachments and know him completely. This is true for everyone, even those who are very close to us and whose lives we know well.

There was only one thing I could say for sure about the person I had just met, and that was that his life there was different and unique. As if he wasn't part of the group of poor people!

He made a place for himself and had a special connection to it. I am not exaggerating if I say that we found almost everything in his closet, from cigars and wine to all kinds of spices and many other surprising things. Let's add this room's nice warmth to the list of things he had.

It was the only place where the big sister and the most experienced monks could enjoy such a luxury. It looks like people in lower ranks were the only ones who had to deal with hardships and hard physical work.

In short, he stayed in a place that made his life easier and more bearable than others. He said his heater was always on and that he had plenty of coffee, cigarettes, and alcohol. He would sometimes flirt with the nuns, which made them feel sexually aroused.

Now, let's talk about his bed and sheets, which were thought to be better than our rough and dry beds.

When I asked him why he got all the benefits and special treatment he did, he said, "There is no specific reason." Maybe it is just because I have a way with their hearts."

Please be honest, there must be another explanation. Is that right?

I don't want to tell you a lie. Because you are my dear guest. If you want to know the truth, I give the big sister a few coins at the end of every month. Yes, I'm talking about gold coins.

Could you tell me where you got the gold coins?

The story is long and full of detail. I'll let you know whenever it's a good time.

I asked her rudely, "Why don't you just say it?"

He thought about it, then said, "Because there's something more important to talk about." I'm talking about how those girls got away. I guess you came here because of that. Don't you?

Do you know anything about them? I tried to talk to some locals today and ask them for some tips. But none of them said anything back.

Nothing is strange, of course. They are so afraid of the big sister that they won't even drink water unless she says so. No one, in particular, should discuss these issues here.

The old man kept talking about the same thing, and I asked, "How do you feel? " "Will they make it across the crossing, or will they die like the others?"

I don't want to make you feel bad or let you down. But I don't think they'll be able to do it. They ran away at a bad time. We can only hope for good luck for them. I wish I was as brave as they were.

I said sarcastically,

Things are not bad for you. So you shouldn't say anything bad.

My words were a bit careless, and it was clear that they hurt him. But he didn't get angry. Instead, he was very calm and said, "Don't judge too quickly, young man." I'm much more upset than you think about what's going on. Believe me, if I could, I wouldn't stay here for a second, and I wouldn't put up with all of this shame.

How come you can't do it? What's holding you back? Do you fear the big sister?

It has nothing to do with fear. I just want this war to end already. I'll leave after this. I don't even look behind me.

What do these things have to do with war?

He hesitated before answering:

"No one here knows I'm wanted." If I leave this "hell of a valley," I will probably be taken to the military court. What if I'm lucky and the Northerners win? Then I can leave this hellhole without getting hurt.

Why did you have to take shelter in such a place?

I pulled a gun on the officer above me. I didn't join because I didn't want to be part of the death squad. I thought you were a bigoted southerner like them.

You must have had this stupid thought because of those medals. You should know that I don't own any of them.

So why did you put them up on the wall? You seem very happy that you have them.

Don't get me wrong, these are just part of my collection.

Do you mean to say that your military record has nothing to do with it?

I'm just a regular sergeant, friend, or maybe I should say I was. I'm not saying that I did nothing wrong. I can make mistakes, just like everyone else. But I'm not the person you think I am. People usually look down on me. I don't blame them, of course. because I've never told anyone about my past.

Can you tell me how you got these medals if that's the case?

Most of them came from officers and veterans who were in bad health. You know better than I do how war changes people.

When you need food and live hand-to-mouth, honors from the past don't mean much and don't matter.

But you still support the people in the South. Don't you?

He gave a very firm and sure answer: "No, not at all." I've had a lot of time to think since I got here. To think about all the things I've relied on my whole life without doing enough research and studying. Now I've realized that I was wrong about a lot of things. Particularly about the ideas and political goals I used to care deeply about.

In other words, my view of the world has changed so much that I can say with certainty that we are now both on the same side.

So we should take it as a good omen.

Now that we know each other better, I hope that as time goes on, our friendship and relationship will grow.

I do as well. How do you feel, my friend?

With a little hesitation, the old man said:

I'm glad to hear that, and I hope this friendship will last forever.

Thanks to you both. Let's drink for our friendship and have fun.

If it's okay with you, I'd rather talk about things that have happened recently.

OK, as you like, my friend. I want to tell you something that will surprise you.

We thought he was going to talk about how those girls got away and what was said about it. But that wasn't the case.

He led us to his room's window and said:

Yesterday, I accidentally found out someone was hiding in the fodder warehouse. First, I decided to go to the big sister and inform her about it. But then I asked myself, "Hey man, what is this?" Do you want to give that poor man the death sentence? In short, I decided to forget about it and not to talk about it until the right time.

What is the appropriate time? Who was hiding there?

So far as I can tell, he is a deserter. If we don't get there quickly to help him, he probably won't survive.

When we heard this, we were a little concerned and shocked. Despite the war's flames reaching the mountain's slopes and spreading day by day, it was very unlikely that a healthy person, let alone someone who was hurt, would go through the crossing and get to the monastery.

But when life or death is at stake, people do things that are beyond their abilities and that they can't do in normal situations.

I am a good example of this human way of dealing with problems and hard times. You have to remember how I went through the heart of this cold, frozen mountain and struggled to get here, coming close to dying several times.

Anyway, this event made us think about something else and temporarily forget about the nuns who were on the run.

In the next part of our conversation, I asked him, "How did you know that he ran away?" Did you talk to him?

Before he answered me, he carefully checked the back of the door to make sure no one was listening. It seems that there were people on the crew and in the monastery who often snitched for the big sister and the people around.

When he got sure about it, he came back to us and told us briefly what had happened.

Then, in response to my previous question, he said:

I could only say a few words to him. He kept passing out, and his words were hard to understand.

What did he say, though?

He said slowly that he was leaving because he had had enough of the war. It looked like soldiers from his side were following him and giving him the wound.

My God, then we'll find them here sooner or later. Didn't he mention his side in the war?

I don't understand what you're talking about!

I'd like to know who we'll be dealing with. From the north or the south side?

Oh, I didn't realize.

What are you saying? You mean he didn't wear any uniforms?

No, he was just wearing a worn-out leather coat. He didn't have anything else with him that showed which side he was on.

So how do you understand that he's telling the truth?

At this moment, the old man got angry with us and what we were talking about, so he spat on both of us and asked:

"Does it matter if it's south or north?" We are humans, and it's our job to run to help him as soon as possible before the big sister and her people find out what happened.

You're right, my friend. We need to work together to figure out what to do.

We were talking about it and making guesses when we heard shouting from inside the area.

We all ran to the window to see what was going on right away. Has anyone heard anything about the girls who ran away and caused so much trouble, or did something else happen? Most of us were worried about that poor soldier who had chosen the worst place to hide. When the big sister's hand reached him, she probably told the colonel about this and asked him to do something about it.

In this case, he will have a very bad and scary ending.

We all knew that if someone left the army during a war, bad things would happen.

If insider forces had caught him, he would have been tried by a military court and probably killed by a death squad. So he would be better off giving up and going to the other side.

Only this way did he have a small chance of saving himself and escaping death. Of course, as long as the big sister and her disciples didn't get their hands on him.

Unfortunately, he was not given the opportunity. They quickly learned of this and discovered where he was hiding. He was cruelly and humiliatingly dragged out of the warehouse and into the monastery right in front of us.

The poor man was moaning and groaning so much that it sounded like he was about to be hanged.

We were very upset by what we saw, and a wave of sadness and anger came over us as a result.

Such a fate wasn't in keeping with a soldier's sense of honor.

Because of his annoyance, our rank-and-file comrade cursed at the big sister, her religion, and her church.

The old man was offended by these words, so he said:

"I hate the big sister just as much as you do. But you shouldn't talk like that about religion and sacred things. This is like a sin!

Sergeant Smith smiled and said, "Oh, you're a good guy!" Which things are sacred? All of these things are a bunch of lies and myths that they told us, poor people, to keep us from thinking about the truth.

Which truth do you want to talk about?

Because there is no heaven or hell, and our fates are all decided here on Earth. In short, whatever you do here, you will reap what you sow.

In other words, religion isn't true at its core. So, you want to say that?

You're merely attempting to appear sophisticated. But you can be sure it doesn't work.

The old man wanted to say something when I interrupted them and asked both of them to finish this discussion.

The host ignored my request and instead asked me:

What are your thoughts on this?

Concerning what? Superstitions?

No. What are your thoughts on religion in general? Are you impious and irreligious like me, or do you truly believe in these things?

I didn't want to aggravate or hurt anyone by continuing this conversation. That's why I responded simply and thoughtfully:

If you ask me, it is not necessary to be bound by a specific religion and ritual to achieve salvation and exaltation of the soul. Only our character and behavior matter. This is also related to social education. It is also the place where we mature and spiritually develop.

This was a summary of my thoughts and beliefs on this matter, which I shared with them candidly and openly in the hope that they would refrain from further discussion. But it didn't happen, and it just added flesh to the bare bones of this debate.

He confirmed my words and added:

In my opinion, religion has impeded science and enlightenment, rather than promoting the growth and development of human societies. Just look at history to see how oppression and cruelty have been inflicted on enlightened and progressive people.

Let us now set aside all of the wars and bloodshed that have occurred in the name of religious expansion. In my opinion, if religion and religious prejudices had not been involved, humanity would have arrived at the gates of science and enlightenment much sooner. However, times have changed, and you must adapt. It is no longer the case that a person is condemned and excommunicated for his or her thoughts and opinions.

What exactly are you saying, old man? Don't you see what the big sister has done to us?

It is not always the case.

It's strange to hear this from someone with your level of experience.

Am I telling the truth?

Such things, in my opinion, happen all over the world. I hope there will come a time when you will be free of this plague. Only then will humanity be able to breathe easily.

Don't be hasty, my friend. I do not deny that religious fanatics are inhumane. Our point of contention is that you are questioning the very essence of religion.

So you don't think I have such a right?

Of course, you do, but only if you keep the side of fairness in mind.

I'm sorry to have to say this. When religious people talk about justice and fairness, it makes me laugh.

Don't be misled. I am not as religious as you believe. Believe me when I say that I violated all religious principles and beliefs. If they understand...

You don't have to go on, my friend. What you said demonstrates that you are also skeptical. You simply do not want to face reality.

Which reality is it?

It is all religions' foundations are built on delusions and superstitions.س

The old man continued, even more, enraged than before:

This is your point of view. Thank goodness, most people don't think that way.

Regrettably, it is the same as you say! However, keep in mind that for nearly two thousand years, most people believed that the earth was the center of the universe and that all planets revolved around it. They also believed in a plethora of other lies and superstitions that are now known to be false.

You're sophisticated.

"Not at all, my friend." This is what religious people always do.

Why do we travel so far? The story of that statue, which you witnessed, is the best example I can give. You can't deny it any longer.

You brought up the subject again. It's as if you want to intentionally hurt me.

What exactly is it, my friend? Perhaps you are afraid of losing your faith. These things do not affect my faith.

This is something I am very familiar with. According to one of my friends, when the subject of religion and religious prejudices is raised, logic and reason are set aside.

The old man was very angry and said, "Watch your mouth." Otherwise, I'll give you whatever comes out of my mouth.

This conversation wasn't going the way it usually did, and it was getting closer and closer to a fight.

I had to find a way to get them to stop thinking about this problem, or else sh*t would hit the fan. But I couldn't do that because I was too curious and I couldn't stop it.

Perhaps you'll ask me how.

Just by asking a simple question:

"What was the story of this statue?"

The old man didn't think I would take the host's side and keep talking about this issue.

He looked at me angrily. Then, with a mad look on his face, he went to the corner of the room and thought about something else.

Just like a child who is upset because his or her parents have scolded and insulted them.

We both had a lot of respect for him, and we didn't want to hurt him in any way, especially in this situation when we needed to be more understanding of each other.

But this conversation had reached a point where I couldn't just ignore it. I wanted to know how and why this story happened.

The host took me behind the window with great enthusiasm and pointed to a spot on the other side of the area, saying, "See that statue over there?" The one who resembles an angel and has wings!

I asked sarcastically, "Have you ever seen an angel with your own eyes know what it looks like?"

He smiled at her and said, "You're right." Out of habit, we sometimes say things that go against what we believe and think. Now, please look closely at that statue and tell me what you think about it.

From what aspect?

I want to know what makes it different from other statues and what makes it unique. From your point of view, of course.

From here, I can't see it very well. We have to get close to it, so I can...

My friend, you can't do it right now.

Why?

We can only get close to the statue on Sundays. If we don't, we'll get in trouble.

You must be joking.

No. I will tell you why in a bit. Now, look at it directly and tell me what you see.

I made my eyes a little sharper and gave a more in-depth opinion. At first glance, I didn't see anything about that statue that stood out or caught my eye.

The statue was cut out of a single piece of white marble. It was the same as the other statues around it, except that it had a large canopy over it.

I was surprised, so I asked,

"What is it about this statue that you like?"

Not a single thing. But some people thought this statue had good qualities and could do miracles. They talked so much about it that they sent people here to check it out.

You must be kidding me. Do you?

One of the sisters said that the statue talked to her, which is impossible.

Oh my goodness! Don't make fun of me.

I'm not joking.

What did it say to her?

He told her about Jesus's pain and suffering that he went through for us. In the end, he had tears coming out of the corners of his eyes.

This is crazy! Who in their right mind would believe something like that?

Then listen to the rest of the story as I tell it. At first, we didn't think much about this problem until the locals told us about it. Then this place got so crowded that you wouldn't believe it.

They came in such large numbers that there wasn't enough room to swing a cat. Of course, it wasn't too bad for us because everyone who came here to make vows and meet needs brought a lot of food and gifts, some of which we got.

Also, I knew from the first day that it smelled like rats. I was just waiting to find a good opportunity to investigate more about this issue more.

I cautiously approached the statue one morning at the crack of dawn and gave it a close inspection.

You have no idea how surprised I was to see that the statue's eyes were wet at the edges. He looked like he was crying.

But I soon figured out why.

In those days, trees and plants of all kinds grew all around the statue. Their leaves covered the statue like an umbrella. I'm not sure if you have heard of morning dew or not.

What happened was that the statue was covered in dew and water vapor.

Then it slowly moves toward the statue's eye, making it look like it is crying. Not a miracle or anything else, just that.

The old man couldn't stand hearing these words, but he didn't say anything. Instead, he walked to the other side of the room and said,

"This is very strange and silly." Who in their right mind would believe this?

Anyone who knows a little bit about science and logic knows that this is possible. Isn't it, my friend?

I think you're right.

You can both say anything you want. I saw things, though, that...

What did you see, for example?

I should say that I saw something with my own eyes. When I was walking by the statue one time, I heard a woman wailing and crying in pain. But when I looked around, I didn't see anyone. As I got closer to the statue, I could hear people talking about some kind of ceremony. So, when I listened, I realized that these whispers are about the time when Jesus was crucified. I'm telling you the truth, so believe me.

I don't think you're hallucinating. But in this case, I have a good reason too.

Ok, tell me, I enjoy listening.

If you remember, I told you at the time that this statue looked hollow. In reality, it is a kind of stone mold that anyone can hide in.

What a waste of time. If you say this, then how do they get in? Don't they use magic to do this?

It's not as hard as you think. If you think about how empty the statue is, you'll see that it's not that hard to shake it off its base. It only takes the power of one or two people. There might be a secret way out of the cellar.

Why should she do something like this? Everyone around respects the big sister so much.

She doesn't have to use these tricks to get what she wants.

Old man, why don't you get it? It's not just the big sister and this monastery that is the problem. The more ignorant and superstitious people are, the stronger the foundations of this intellectual system become.

This is good for all the people who use this blessed table for their good. Take it from His Excellency the Pope and those fat-bellied bishops at the Vatican to...

You went too far when you said that all religious people are hypocrites and believe in silly things.

You can keep fooling yourself with these words, but I've known for a long time what religion is.

I'm sorry, I didn't know you were Mr. Know It All.

Friends, please. Instead of saying these words, it would be better to think about that poor soldier before it's too late.

Unfortunately, we can't do anything special about it. Let's wait and see what they decide to do.

What are you talking about? You and I were soldiers too! Because of this, we shouldn't be so blasé about our fellow soldiers.

We don't know which group or side he belongs to. He might be a bad and sneaky person.

In any case, he is a person who needs help right away. You didn't see how he was whining and complaining. Think about it from his point of view for a minute, and...

You are right. But for now, you shouldn't do anything about this.

I didn't expect you to be so scared of the big sister. We're talking about the life of a soldier.

I am not just thinking about what might happen to us. I'm afraid that if we help, the big sister will get mad and make things worse for the soldier.

I feel terrible. I think this is an attempt to explain and justify.

So, old man, what do you think?

If that soldier is smart and shows that he is a stubborn and loyal Christian, he might be able to change the big sister's mind.

If he is not a Protestant. If he is, his situation will be worse.

So we have to meet him where he is and make him feel like he should do what is to his benefit.

If you ask me, the best thing to do is to put a cross around his neck and some prayer sheets in his pocket. How do you feel about this?

It's a good idea, but it's already too late.

Why?

I'm sure they've already taken off all of his clothes and looked everywhere. After all, the big sister is too smart to be fooled by these things.

I'm sure she will ask him a lot of questions to find out if he believes what he says or if he's just making it up.

So something like this has already happened here?

Since we've been here, at least five or six people have taken shelter in the monastery. The last one was a scammer named Thomas who seemed to be running away from his creditors.

When he got here, he talked and told stories about the Bible in a way that made everyone take notice.

But they soon caught him while he was stealing some expensive statues.

What did they do with him, though?

First, they put him in the basement and tortured him a lot. His groans and cries have not yet left my ears, yet I can still hear them. The next morning, some of the village's elders and those who had complained about that man came here.

He was tried quickly, and then he was put to death without being able to say anything in his defense.

God, I don't know how this woman can do such things.

That's not important. A few years ago, several people were found guilty of atheism and witchcraft and put to death.

You might not believe it, but at first, they wanted to put them in a fire while they were still alive. But they were very lucky that the big sister was kind to them. If she hadn't, they would have endured excruciating pain and suffering in their final moments.

Yes, you're right. It's hard to believe. It felt like I went through a made-up gate and into the Middle Ages.

If you ask me, these kinds of things will keep happening as long as there is ignorance and superstition in the world. So you shouldn't be too shocked by this. I wish I could just stay in Arkansas and stay out of this stupid war. I wouldn't be stuck in this purgatory.

That means you're from there. I've heard that's where the most extreme Southerners live. Is that right?

Do not believe everything you hear, my friend. Everywhere, there are both good and bad people. Aren't there?

Curse on the deniers. But the problem is that the bottom of the scale is heavier on the second side! Now, let's move on to this subject. Could you tell me what you were doing there?

I had good land and fields until the river flooded and made it impossible for me to keep working.

I'm sorry. You must have decided to join the army after this happened.

No, I worked on a steamship for a few years before that. I wasn't in such a bad spot before I thought about joining the army.

So it wasn't because of what you believed in?

To be honest, I had habits and ideas at that time that led me in the wrong direction. But as time went on, I saw that I had made the wrong choice.

What are you going to do now? You want to stay here forever and think about the bad things that have happened.

Of course not. I am waiting to see how this war ends. I've already said that if the internal forces catch me, I'll probably be tried and punished.

So, I hope that the northerners will win, have grace, and forgive. I've heard that some of them are very good and fair.

Does that mean you don't have any family, friends, or other people waiting for you?

Yes, I do. I have a lot of family and friends there. But the place and nature I left behind are what I miss the most.

You don't know what a pleasure it is to hear that beautiful river whisper (the Mississippi River).

Especially at night, when you sat around the fire and forgot about all the chaos and conflict around you.

I wouldn't have left for anything if I'd known how valuable these seemingly insignificant things would turn out to be. Worse, if I had the right goals and ideals, I wouldn't get into trouble like this.

I know what you're trying to say, but you shouldn't feel guilty. At least you were brave enough to admit you were wrong and choose a different path.

I'm sure you'll get out of this hellhole and get on with your life sooner or later.

He smiled and said,
My friend, this hope keeps me alive.

Chapter Six: The Evil Day

When my friends came up to me with sad faces and very bad news, I was shaving my face. Sadly, none of the girls were able to get away. I had already planned for something like this to happen and was ready for it. So, I wasn't too surprised. Every smart and sensible person knew that it was almost impossible to get through that crossing in those conditions.

It was something that could only be done by people who were healthy and strong. They also need to bring enough tools and supplies. If they don't, their lives will depend on luck and maybes.

The poor old man was very upset and blamed himself for everything.

He was about to burst into tears. It was like he had lost someone he cared about.

Anyway, what's done is done, and sighing and wishing things were different didn't help.

We were talking about this problem and trying to figure out how to solve it when we heard drums and other noises not too far away. It felt like a huge and powerful army was coming at us.

The sound made the old man shake, and he said:

"They've arrived. I knew this was the end. I just want to know if they're still alive."

The old man then left the room quickly. We followed him too, hoping to find both of them still alive.

Even though the poor girls were going to get a harsh and painful punishment, it was better than dying this way.

When we got to the yard, the big sister and a group of her followers were waiting by the gate.

She couldn't hide her happiness from the look of pride on her face or the smile on her lips.

I was so mad at her at the time that I wanted to find a way to turn her off and let her know that she would have to pay for her actions someday.

Others felt more or less like me. But there wasn't much we could do besides give them cold, hateful looks.

We stayed like this for a short time in the cold and icy weather until we saw the dark shapes of a few people in the distance.

Their movements and actions were not too different from those of soldiers coming home from war. They were making a lot of noise and shouting as if they had just won a great victory.

When they got a little closer, we all saw a very bitter and horrible truth.

They were carrying the bodies of those innocent girls. There was no doubt about that.

They threw the bodies on the mule in a disgusting and humiliating way, and then went back to their lord and guardian with proud looks on their faces.

In the back of their minds, they probably thought that they deserved their big sister's praise and the reward in the afterlife.

No one could have hoped for more from this group of uneducated and fanatical people.

They'd do anything to make their big sister happy. From killing and robbing to torturing people with different ideas and thoughts.

They thought that what they were doing was God's will and providence, and they did not feel bad or ashamed about it. Instead, they were happy and content in their hearts. In this kind of situation, no one in the monastery could cry and mourn.

If they did that, they would be reprimanded and blamed for being suspected of cooperating with or even showing sympathy for those fugitives. One could only get a sense of how people felt from the way they looked and how they were acting.

Some people looked like they didn't care at all and were acting as if nothing had happened. On the other hand, some people were severely hurt by this incident, including me and my friends.

The very least we could do was get to the bottom of this story and learn more about their deaths.

Who knows, maybe there will be a chance to bring these people to court in the future. In that case, our testimony would be extremely valuable and significant. But first, I had to carefully examine the bodies to determine the cause of death. It goes without saying that I was not extremely inexperienced and untrained in this field. At the beginning of my service in the army, I had the chance to work with an elite police officer who was investigating the murder of a high-ranking officer.

It was a very significant and beneficial experience in my life, and I am now reaping the benefits. But I needed to hurry. They needed to move the bodies to the cellar. In that case, I wouldn't be able to thoroughly check and analyze them.

I was thinking about this problem when I had some unexpected luck.

The big sister requested that her people position the bodies in front of us more clearly. She meant to hurt us and show those who were thinking of running away or fighting her a lesson.

It was a terrible decision that demonstrated this person's prejudice and cruelty.

She was so sure of herself that she never imagined she would be accused and tried for her actions.

In any case, it provided me with an excellent opportunity to examine the bodies.

At first glance, it looked like they had both died from the cold. The way their faces looked and how still they were made me think of the statues that were set up in the corners of the monastery. It was as if new bodies were being brought as gifts and offerings to the big sister. But it was impossible to say for sure that nothing else bad had happened to them. They have bruises on their hands and faces that don't look like they were caused by frostbite. They most certainly did not permit any of us to investigate and examine this issue further. Even a casual conversation or comment on this issue could be extremely costly.

It's not too much of an exaggeration to say that this place was like a huge black hole that swallowed and erased all important human values and standards at once.

It was hard for me to see things like that.

On the one hand, I was looking at the dead bodies of people who had gone through such terrible things to get their freedom and natural rights. On the other hand, I was living with a monster who was overjoyed to see this sight and kept looking at it with an insatiable hunger. The big sister was like someone who enjoys humiliating her enemies and haters.

Now I know that getting rid of this evil and cursed place won't be easy.

They wanted us to understand that the only way out of this horrible hell is to embrace death.

It was the fate of everyone who was trapped in this medieval crypt.

I was not the type of person who would bear the humiliation and do nothing about it. I also had ideas in my head that, if carried out, would lead to my and others' being free of this disgusting place.

I just needed a little more time, as well as the assistance and cooperation of my friends, to put this plan into action.

***

That night, the bodies were buried. Of course, it was already known that no one would be permitted to examine the bodies or do additional research. However, we did not expect this to be completed so quickly and without a formal ceremony.

The haste with which they buried the bodies indicated that their deaths were caused by something other than an accident and frostbite.

We were all sure that those two nuns had been badly hurt, sexually assaulted, and physically tortured.

If this story spread, it would undoubtedly harm and taint the purity of the big sister and this ostensibly hallowed site.

She was unconcerned about the people in this neighborhood. As I previously stated, the majority of them agreed with her thoughts and beliefs and dispelled any doubts about her.

Even if she was allowed to attack and disrespect the most important people in the village, they still found a way to explain and justify her actions!

Her worry and anxiety mostly came from the fact that the war was getting bigger and bigger, as well as the huge political and cultural changes that could spread there and force them to face the harsh consequences of their actions.

Perhaps her encounter with someone like me made her more cautious and foresighted than before.

That night, something else important and fateful happened, and I'll tell you all about it.

It was early in the evening when the old man approached me gloomily and asked me to spend an hour with him and another of our mutual friends.

I gladly accepted his invitation as well. We were all upset about the incident and were trying to console each other in some way. At the same time, we were trying to figure out how to get out of this difficult situation.

If we simply ignore this horrible incident, we will face another bitter and shocking incident sooner or later. There was no question about it.

As a result, we should have disgraced the big sister and her people in every way possible and prevented these crimes from continuing.

We'd be considered accomplices otherwise.

We were discussing and plotting this relationship when the door to the room suddenly opened, and the big sister stepped inside with a distracted expression and a weapon in her hand.

For a brief moment, we considered that the final chapter of our lives had arrived.

We probably encouraged the big sister to do such a bad job because of our constant curiosity and the way we behaved. But why did she need to do this herself?

Just a hint from her was enough for her followers to simply delete us all from all of existence, leaving no trace of any of us behind.

While we stood there dumbfounded, she came a little closer and said quietly and tremblingly:

"Some strange men are inside the yard." I believe they have ill will toward us.

On the one hand, this word made us feel at ease, but on the other, it caused us to be concerned and anxious.

Maybe these people were looking for the fugitive soldier. They had nothing to do with others in this case.

There was also the possibility that they had nefarious plans.

Assaulting women and stealing food and valuables were among the most heinous crimes they could commit. We were all well aware that such incidents were common during wartime.

If it happened, we would have no choice but to fight back and protect the people who live in the monastery.

We despised and despised the big sister, but our humanity, honor, and duty demanded that we protect her and the other residents of the monastery.

Let us not forget that our lives were in danger as well. We were the only ones who could provide some protection to the monastery and its residents. The rest of the men had returned to the village, their jobs, and their lives, leaving the monastery staff with little to do because the majority of them were sick or disabled, such as the hunchbacked man who mistreated me when I first arrived at the monastery.

It was for this reason that the big sister came to us right away.

She handed me the weapon and told me not to let them into the hall at any cost.

I first checked to see if the weapon was ready to fire.

When I was certain, I asked her:

"If a conflict arises, can we use weapons safely?" "Is it possible that we get into trouble later on because of that?"

But the big sister assured us that it would not be the case. She then said a prayer and exited the room. It was so quick and hasty that there was no time for further questions or exploration.

When she left, I warned my friends to be cautious and keep an eye out. The big sister's behavior made me extremely skeptical.

She didn't value any of our lives, and she didn't mind getting rid of all three of us in some way. In this particular case, all three of us agreed.

So she could have used us as bait and sacrificial meat.

Although it was unfortunate for her that something bad had happened to us if not, it was unknown what would happen to her and the other monastery residents. Of course, this assumes she hasn't set a trap for us.

We quickly discovered that there are no tricks and that the threat is real.

When we looked out of the window on the second floor, we saw people we didn't know looking for a way into the monastery.

The majority of their focus was on the side where the sisters were staying. It appeared that the woman's pleasant odor reached their noses and intoxicated them. Their actions indicated that they are already familiar with the coordinates of this building and are not playing games. However, it appears that it is still too early to pass judgment on this matter.

Perhaps, contrary to popular belief, they were not thinking evil thoughts and were simply looking for a safe and warm place to spend the night on this cold and stormy night. In this case, with a little food and entertainment from the monks, everything would be fine. But I quickly got rid of that ridiculous thought.

What was the point of acting so loudly and suspiciously if they had no bad intentions? So they had negative thoughts.

With a little effort, they could step over the fence and into the open area.

The main issue was getting into the building.

Every night, after the bell rang at the appointed time, all doors and windows were closed and locked from the inside.

A thick and very strong fence stood in front of each of the windows, blocking the entrance in this way.

The main door was also designed so that it could only be removed and destroyed by a cannonball. In short, we were in a good and safe place that wasn't too different from a military fort.

They could only get into the monastery if someone from inside helped them or if they were very good at what they were doing.

We were assessing the situation and exchanging ideas when we heard someone's feet and movement downstairs. Unless a special event or an unavoidable necessity occurred,

none of the crew had the right to leave their rooms at such an   hour.
They couldn't even leave their rooms to deal with nature and issues like this! Only the big sister and the great nuns could stand up to these absurd and irrational rules. Her greatest fear and concern, if you ask me, were the sexual and erotic issues that involved the minds of the nuns and other members of the monastery, whether they wanted it or not.

No matter how many fences and walls they built to keep them apart, it was still impossible to stop and restrain the outburst and excitement of this natural desire. It was an undeniable fact that these people couldn't digest or accept. Aside from that, that night we were all confronted with a serious and common danger that could cost us our lives.

The thing that frightened and worried me the most was that someone from within would come to the aid of those unknown people and open the door for them. In this case, there would be a bloody and lethal clash between us. We should have ensured this before proceeding.

Let's not act too quickly and wake up the other people in the monastery, who were sleeping and didn't know what was going on.

I went ahead of my friends to the stairs and looked down the hall.

The space below was so dark that I couldn't see anything clearly, but something inside me told me that something dangerous might be there.

At the same time, there was a strange noise coming from downstairs. My time in the military taught me to stay calm and cool in these kinds of situations.

I went down a few steps and looked at the four corners of the hall while I was getting ready to shoot.

My friends also moved slowly and carefully behind me.

We've all been on battlefields and fought in bloody wars, more or less. But we were a little scared and worried.

This confrontation was very different from what we had done before, and each of us had to be very brave to get through it.

When we got to the bottom of the stairs, we saw something that stopped us all in our tracks. Someone from inside came to help the strangers and opened the door for them, which was a bad thing. Now, our lives were all in very real danger. I promised myself right away that if we got out of this situation alive, I would find this person and teach him a good lesson in any way I could.

There were three people who attacked. It gave us the chance to be better than them. One of them, who was tall and fit, was standing at the door with his back to the others and a hostile look on his face. Two of them were a meter behind him. They all had weapons and were ready to fight. Now it's clear that they want to do bad things.

In this situation, it seemed like a fight was going to happen unless one side showed weakness and stepped back.

We didn't mean to do that. They also seemed sure of themselves and sure enough not to care about such a possibility.

If we had acted first and taken up arms sooner, we might have been able to stop the attackers.

They were stronger and had better weapons and ammunition than us. On the other hand, we were in a better position than they were.

I was standing behind a statue near the stairwell, my finger on the trigger, ready to shoot.

My friends had also gone to a safe and convenient place to wait for the fighting to start.

Because I was the only one armed among them, they expected a quick and calculated reaction from me.

I was familiar with a variety of weapons and other war tools.

I also won a shooting competition between army units that are held every year, which was very important. However, due to unforeseen circumstances, I was unable to fully utilize my abilities in this field. In addition to the weakness and illness that affected my mental accuracy and concentration, anxiety and stress exacerbated the problem and severely depleted my ability, not to mention that I lacked a lethal weapon. There were too few bullets. I couldn't possibly resist them for long in these circumstances. In this case, I would also jeopardize the lives of others.

Sergeant Smith was fully aware of what was going on.

He requested that I give him the weapon so that he could bear this heavy and vital responsibility on his own. My natural pride, however, would not permit it. I was determined to show everyone my bravery and readiness while cracking the whip on the attackers.

I yelled:

"You better not move, you bastard, or I'll shoot each of you."

It was not an exaggerated or meaningless threat. However, it had little impact on the attackers' lives in terms of fear and anxiety. They knew we weren't as well armed or prepared for a fight as they were.

If they hadn't, they wouldn't have lined up in front of us so recklessly and easily.

I needed to act quickly so that they would take us seriously and not pursue us any further. We would be the ultimate losers in this conflict if we did not do so.

Moments passed in agonizing silence before one of the attackers summoned the courage to draw a weapon. I, too, fired without hesitation at him.

I'm not sure if it was luck or skill, but my bullet hit exactly where I wanted it to and knocked him out cold.

The other two returned. In the blink of an eye, they fled to a different area of the monastery's grounds.

They unleashed a hail of aimless bullets on us after a brief respite, but none of them struck us. It only harmed the door, the wall, and the statues.

To keep our advantage, we needed to keep the attackers out of the monastery as soon as possible.

It was not an easy task. They continued to shoot at the door and refused to let any of us pass. We'd have a much better chance of defeating them if we could get our hands on the weapons and ammunition that the fallen soldier had left behind.

The sergeant and I tried a few times but were unsuccessful. We nearly died while doing this.

The bullet abrasion on the sergeant's shoulder and scapula caused a small scratch on the skin. I was unlucky enough to be injured in my right arm. Fortunately, these injuries were not severe enough to render us immobile.

While we were stuck, the old man made a sudden and unexpected movement, which surprised both of us.

He jumped down from the top of the stairs and into the corner of the hall, like a quick and lively youth. The location was out of reach of the attackers.

The old man then crawled to the door and struggled to close it. As bullets whizzed past and over his head, he dropped the door's iron latch.

This move was so daring and unexpected that it caught both of our breaths.

He walked up to the man's body calmly and coldly and took his gun and ammunition after blocking their way in.

I'm not sure where he got all of his courage and self-assurance. Was his faith in life so weak that he had no fear of death, or was his innate bravery to blame? Whatever his motivation, he had rekindled the flame of hope in all of our hearts with this action. I'd even venture to say that it saved the entire monastery's population.

They were terrified and crawled to the corner of their rooms, praying for the danger to leave them alone, unaware that prayer does not heal either us or them. It was only a temporary source of comfort and peace for their hearts. If we, like them, relied on prayer and looked to the sky, we would undoubtedly meet a terrible end. As a result, leaving this group victorious was in their best interests; otherwise, no other force could have reached them.

We waited 30 minutes to see what would happen. Do the attackers miss the appeal of this colorful and whimsical table and abandon us, or do they have other plans? Meanwhile, we visited the big sister and some of the nuns and made them feel comfortable and uplifted.

Nobody bothered us to go to other parts of the monastery because of what happened that night.

So we roamed freely in the territory of the big sister, and I took advantage of the opportunity.

At the same time, we took turns patrolling the perimeter.

We'd probably get rid of these people if we could hold out until dawn like this.

Every morning, a group of villagers came to the monastery for pilgrimage, to obtain religious duties, and to meet and talk with the big sister. Some of them also assisted the crew with their daily tasks.

It was extremely unlikely that anyone would want to attack the monastery and its residents under these circumstances unless he was unfamiliar with the area.

Anyway, as midnight approached, we began to notice suspicious movements around the building. The attackers appeared to be looking for another way into the monastery.

Our main concern was the person who had previously prepared the way for these people to enter the monastery, and we still had no idea who he was.

In this situation, the best we could do was ring the bell and notify the people of the nearby village that something bad had occurred.

As I had heard, they had a special sign for these occasions, similar to Morse code!

The old man consulted with the big sister on our behalf to get approval for the proposed action. But, for some reason we don't know, she turned it down!

The only option left to us was to reinforce the door and windows so that the attackers could not gain entry. Others concurred with me.

There was also the hope that the sound of successive gunshots would reach the villagers' ears and direct them in this direction.

So we should encourage the attackers to attack again. When they started working and fired a wave of bullets at the door and windows, we were thinking the same thing.

It didn't help them at all, and all it did was scare and worry the nuns and other people who lived in the monastery. They had never been through something so terrible before.

The attackers should have known that the building's main frame is very strong and hard to break through and that these shots won't do much damage to it unless they use gunpowder and heavy bullets.

After shooting for ten minutes straight, they did something none of us saw coming.

They continued swinging around, burning objects around their heads and throwing them at us. When these fireballs hit the door and windows, they caught fire quickly.

People were really worried that the fire would spread to other parts of the monastery and take everyone with it.

I was so enraged by this heinous and cruel act that I yelled and ran out of the monastery without thinking.

I repeatedly shot around aimlessly at the same time. They responded by doing the same.

I was fortunate not to be seriously injured. Only a small piece of glass and a wood chip got stuck in my foot, which wouldn't have happened if I was wearing shoes. A lot was going on in the monastery at the time. It was almost like a battle scene.

My friends were working hard to stop the fire from getting into the building, while screams and moans could be heard from every direction.

Now it was my job to stand up to the attackers and not let them use this situation to their advantage. The clumsy encounter I had with them a few minutes ago helped me figure out where they were hiding. One of them was hiding behind some big, heavy barrels near the fodder feed barn, which was thought to be a good and fairly strong fortress. The other one also got to the well and was hiding behind the arch and its wall, which wasn't very high.

They were on both sides of me and kept firing at me. I could only beat these trained and professional soldiers if my friends put out the fire inside the monastery as quickly as possible and came to help me.

In this situation, someone else came along and changed things right away in our favor.

In that darkness, I couldn't see his face very well.

It didn't matter.

It was important to take advantage of this good chance and kill at least one of the intruders. The unknown man acted quickly and killed the person hiding behind the barrels with a blow from a scythe or something similar. It is more accurate to say that he tore him apart. I have never come up behind someone and killed him in such a cruel way. I don't think this kind of fight has anything to do with human dignity. But when there is war, it is very hard to stick to these principles and values, and it can even cost you your life.

After all, we were up against people who didn't care about honor or humanity, or else they wouldn't have done such horrible things. They had done terrible things in the past. So there was no reason to feel sorry for or care about them.

I finally hurt the other intruder enough to push him back a little bit. But he made it to the stable and stayed there for the night, even though it didn't look like he could stand up to us anymore. He was stuck like a mouse and couldn't do anything out of the ordinary.

I was walking slowly toward the stable when a man I didn't know came out of the darkness and showed me his face.

He was tall and charming, and he had the look of a winner.

Unconsciously, I was scared, and I got ready to shoot to protect myself, thinking that he was having a bad dream.

He put his weapon down quickly and put both hands up as if he were giving up!

Then he told me to calm down and let him tell me who he was. I did the same thing with some doubt.

He must have had permission from the court to take these people into custody and give them to the court.

It seems that these three people, whether they are alive or dead, have set a huge reward that could make anyone want to help.

I asked him to prove what he said was true by showing me his warrant and license. He did the same thing, which made me feel a lot better.

We were very lucky that he was able to find them and get to us right when we needed him the most. But we still had more work to do.

We had to get that jerk out of the stable and finish his work in any way we could. We didn't want the animals in the stable to get hurt. So, we waited a little bit and didn't act too quickly.

We were talking about this and sharing our thoughts and ideas when we heard the sound of people fighting inside. It looked like someone else was in the stable with the attacker, and they got into a fight.

But who could that man be? It went on for a few minutes until we heard a faint but very sad moan.

We were let into the stable a little while later. If I tell you who came in front of us, you might be surprised.

You must recall the hunchbacked man. He'd slashed the last attacker's throat with a rake and put us at ease.

Now I can confidently say that this conflict has ended in our favor. However, it was not yet clear how much damage and casualties we had sustained.

This incident woke some people up and made them realize that the fires of war had finally reached this remote location.

Everything changed after this incident, and the situation did not return to its previous state. I only hoped that this transformation would result in positive changes.

6.1. The Following Morning

All the people in the monastery worked together to clean up after the fight the night before and get things back to how they were.

We were the only ones who didn't have to do this hard work, so we stayed in our rooms and took it easy.

The selflessness and bravery we showed the night before were important and powerful enough to win the big sister's forgiveness and favor.

From the way the sisters looked at us and talked to each other, it was clear that they were very interested in us, especially me, who was younger and more active than the others.

After eating a fancy breakfast that was made just for us, I went back to my room and rested like a person who had been treated well.

It didn't take long for my eyelids to get heavy, and I was soon ready for a long, deep sleep. Someone entered my room without my permission at this time and crept up on tiptoes to my bed.

I was so tired and worn out that I didn't feel like talking to anyone. So, I acted as if I was sleeping, not knowing that the big sister had come to see me.

I knew who it was when the big sister gently asked me, "Are you awake?"

Her voice sounded very different at that moment. It felt like a close friend and companion had come up to me and asked how I was.

Surely, she was so kind and gentle because of the self-sacrifice that I made the night before. But I didn't answer her so I could get rid of her as quickly as possible.

But then something happened that I had no idea would happen, and it surprised me.

The big sister slowly leaned over me and gave me a soft kiss on the arm, thinking I was fast asleep.

She also ran her fingers through my hair. It seemed like all of a sudden, her sexual desires and motivations woke up, and she came out of the crazy world of celibacy and physical mathematics.

In any case, this physical contact came out of the blue and was both comforting and pleasurable. It made me catch my breath for a moment.

Let me tell you the truth. I used to make a lot of claims about it and talk a lot about it. I'm referring to sexual encounters and relationships with women. But when it came to the act, I was so tense and anxious that I used any excuse and pretext to let go and avoid it.

It was unusual for a woman to give me such comfort and assurance that I would not fall into such a state.

Certainly, the big sister was not one of them.

I didn't mind sleeping with her or flirting with her.

If that were true, she would no longer be able to attack me and demonstrate her false sanctity. I was having the same thoughts and dreams when I heard chattering and talking from the back of the room.

The big sister was so terrified and startled that she thought the angel of death had appeared to her. If someone saw her in this state above my head, he might think negatively and awkwardly about her.

She remained there for a few moments until things returned to normal. She then left me alone with my thoughts and imagination.

I have to say that this unexpected event made me less angry and hateful toward the big sister, and it gave me hope that she might change the way she thinks and acts.

To be honest, I was more interested in the sexual side of this issue. I like to sleep with someone who had never had natural sex or made love and was just starting in this world had a taste and charm that could easily provoke and tempt anyone. Naturally, assuming her claim of avoiding sex and practicing physical abstinence is true.

Anyway, I stayed in bed that day until about noon and got a lot of rest.

Then, my friends and I helped the people who were still cleaning the monastery and the area around it. Some people from the village joined us in the afternoon and took over the rest of the work.

They brought all the tools and equipment they would need as if they were already ready for something like it to happen.

One of them had to fix the windows and put in new panes of glass. Others also put the bodies in the cart, along with the weapon, all of the bullets, and anything else that was needed to find out who the attackers were and report the attack to the police.

After the work was done, they made a big meal for us all and thanked each of us in the right way.

The big sister thought that by acting this way, she could make up for her bad and crazy behavior and make us forget about the real world, but it never works. We couldn't turn away from the heartbreaking death of those innocent girls and try to hide from the truth.

If we did that, we would feel ashamed and regretful for the rest of our lives, and we would no longer be able to hold our heads high with pride and respect morality and humanity.

Strange things happen, and things go up and down all the time in life. I never thought I'd be in this kind of situation a year ago.

I'd gone to this remote location in the hopes of healing and getting away from the dreadful atmosphere of the war, not realizing I'd stepped onto a more dangerous path. I was grateful to have some good and trustworthy friends by my side, on whom I could rely in difficult times; otherwise, I would not have been able to bear this situation. This event brought us three closer together, so much so that people joked about us being the Three Musketeers.

When I was in such a bad mood and situation, the thought of sleeping with the big sister became more real to me and took up most of my thoughts.

I had no idea what would happen at the end. Would I be able to get closer to her and have sexual relations with her, or would I end up in even more trouble?

The only way to find out was to set aside my fear and doubt and give it a shot.

That night, ironically, I had a very good and unexpected opportunity that put my determination to achieve this goal to the test.

While I was getting ready for bed, the old man approached me with zeal and said,

"Put on your clothes quickly and come with me." "I'm going to show you something you won't believe."

I asked, coldly and sarcastically,

"What happened that got you so excited?" "Is it a miracle that we are unaware of?"

He sat on the edge of the bed next to me and said, "If you ask me, it's a miracle." I wouldn't be so shocked if the moon fell from the sky, believe me.

"Don't go out of your way to tell me what happened."

"I don't know where the sun is today, because the big sister is being so loving and kind. Surely, it is due to what we did last night. "Is it not?"

"Don't be crazy, my friend. This group, which I know, doesn't love people for no reason, let alone people like us, whom they consider to be atheists. "Tell me what she did that made you so happy."

"Each of us got a bottle of wine from our older sister." "What an honest wine!"

"Just this?!"

"Now I'll say the rest." She came up to us and told us to have a party tonight in the courtyard. "Some dancers and musicians were also invited to this party from the village."

"You know what I mean. Tonight is one of those nights when anything could happen."

"You're such a simple man, old man. She is taking advantage of this situation to help herself.

"Why?"

"So that everything looks normal." In reality, she wants us to forget about what happened to those poor girls."

"She did something very wrong." Is it possible to forget it so quickly? When the time comes, I promise to teach her a good lesson. But it's not a bad idea to use it to your advantage. As everyone knows, some sisters want things very badly. "We might be able to do something out of sight of the big sister."

"Don't say that you didn't come up with it on your own."

I showed no interest in this matter and did not discuss it further. But he figured out what I was thinking.

***

We joined the people at the monastery as they danced and laughed.

When I looked into the nuns' eyes, they couldn't help but react, which showed that their sexual and emotional needs were aroused.

Believe me, if I put my hands on any of them, they would quickly give in and fit in my arms. But none of them caught my attention.

I thought about flirting with someone they couldn't even think of.

We stayed like this for half an hour until the big sister came back. As soon as they saw her, the nuns moved back and kept their distance from us. With just one look at everyone, their happy, lively faces turned cold and soulless, and they took on a holy, innocent look.

By making a sign, the big sister told them to feel at ease.

like a queen who treats her maids and servants with grace and care. Then she went to the fire and shared her joy with the other people there. Of course, in a way that doesn't hurt its religious authority or holiness too much.

At the same time, as I stood right in front of her, she gave me a special, lustful look.

At that moment, both of our lives were on fire, and sparks were flying out every second.

Both of us had no choice but to give in to this intense physical desire. Also, the conditions were set up well.

The big sister did something on purpose to get people's attention away from us. She let everyone stay up late, drink as much wine as they wanted, and have a good time. She sent only a few of the youngest sisters and nuns to the dormitory before the others, depriving them of this unexpected grace and mercy.

She didn't want this situation to lead to something she would later regret.

When everyone was drunk and acting crazy, she left the crowd slowly and went to the feed barn. At the same time, she looked at me once or twice and smiled in a way that made me want to be with her—those smiles that make even a stone heart melt.

I had thought about this scene many times before.

Since the first time we met and talked, this thought has been stuck in my head like a gnat and won't go away. Now I had the chance, to tell the truth about my fantasies and hit this woman's endless pride and arrogance where it hurt. But I was still unsure and scared, and I didn't want to take the last step.

I was scared and worried for a good reason.

She could easily grab me, put out the fire of her desire, and then get rid of me without much trouble.

I even worried that all these smiles, tricks, and charms were just lies and ruses.

Was she trying to get back at me for our disagreements and different ways of thinking, or was she just burning with lust and desires she couldn't express? Only one thing could make sure of it. I had to put my natural shyness and fear aside and go after her. If not, I would be sad for the rest of my life that I missed this chance!

I stayed there for a few minutes while waiting for everything to be ready.

Then I carefully put some distance between myself and my friends and went to the feed store. I kept looking behind me to see if anyone was paying attention. Everyone was too busy drinking to pay attention to me, though. I thought so, at least.

I didn't see anyone in the feed barn when I went in. At first, I thought that maybe I was wrong about what was going on and what I thought it meant.

It means there was a chance I could have been wrong! At that moment, the only answer I could think of was "not at all."

I had so much experience that I knew exactly what a woman wanted and needed sexually and didn't mess up. But I couldn't just ignore another assumption. She may have fought off her sexual urge at the last second and gone back.

How, though?

I saw her go into the feed barn with my own eyes. I was sure she wouldn't come out of there.

No one could get in or out any other way. So I knew she would be waiting somewhere for me.

I was thinking about this when I heard something move in the feed barn's upper level. At that time, both the feed barn staff and the delivery men were having fun in the area. So for sure, no one else but the big sister could be up there.

Even though I had been preparing for this moment, I still felt fear and anxiety, and I stood still for a few seconds. It didn't come as a surprise at all.

You will probably have reservations about having sexual relations and sleeping with someone who is a saint to everyone else and will do anything for her unless you have already given a lot.

The big sister wasn't in as much danger as I was, and she could easily get away from the worst accusations.

No one would have the guts to ask her a question because she was so holy and respected.

Assuming it's not possible if someone heard about it and tried to tell others, no one would believe him. He was eventually charged with and sentenced for lying and slander.

Let's keep going even if the whole truth was told to everyone else. That is, they were sure that we were seeing each other and having sexual relations. Again, she wasn't in much danger.

You might ask how.

She was able to say that I insulted her and made her sit on something dirty against her will. In this case, I knew a bad and very scary thing was going to happen.

In general, they accepted every reason and excuse she gave without question or suspicion as if she had never done anything wrong.

I have dealt with people like this. So, one small mistake and lack of care were all it took for all of them to fall on me and end my lineage.

Logic and reason told me to take a few minutes and think carefully about the end of my work again. I did the same thing, by the way. But in the end, my lust and desire to be rebellious won out over my reason and wisdom and made me want to keep going down this path.

I climbed the ladder and got to the top of the feed barn, even though I was very nervous.

Something was waiting for me that I had already fantasized about.

The big sister was naked and lying in the dry grass like a baby who had just been born.

Now I knew for sure that she had given herself up to me completely and without any strings attached. But her face showed that she was worried and stressed out. She was so embarrassed by me that she couldn't even look me in the eyes.

It was a perfectly reasonable and fair thing to do. What you don't know is that my mood and day were not much different from hers.

I looked at her for a few seconds without moving. It felt like all of my muscles had gone paralyzed.

I still couldn't understand or believe that she had changed so quickly.

What changed her in this strange and unexpected way? I asked myself this question over and over. But I still hadn't found an answer that was right and made sense.

After a short delay and some waiting, I moved and slowly walked toward her.

It was the first time she got close to someone and had a sexual encounter. So I had to pay close attention. Lest she goes through more fear and worries and leaves me wanting what she wants.

I laid still next to her for a few minutes so she could calm down a bit.

The sound of her strong, lustful breaths got me even more excited and ready to get close to her. I still waited for her to make the first move, though.

Aside from these things, I have to say that she had a very beautiful and hypnotic body.

I had no idea that that rough black cover was hiding such a priceless gem. She had a lean and fit body as a result of her strict physical austerities and constant abstinence. Maybe she had such a characteristic by nature.

In general, I liked women who were slim and small more.

Perhaps because most of the women I admired possessed this or a similar trait, such as my dear and lovely adopted mother and Aunt Maria, or my attractive and passionate cousins who I had no idea where they were. But it wasn't the only thing about the sister's naked body that caught my eye and made my heart beat faster.

I couldn't stop looking at how beautiful and well-shaped her breasts were. The best way I can describe those two beautiful clusters is by saying they were almost perfect.

It was a shame that she kept this heavy veil over her body for so many years and didn't use it to its full potential.

You might think that I am a capricious and unrestrained person. If not, I wouldn't have been so open with you about such things. But the truth is very different.

The only reason I'm writing it is to explain everything that happened to me during that cold and tiring winter.

I also think that by doing it, you will learn more about my interests and moods. So, if you don't mind, please stay with me until the end of this story and try not to be biased.

The big sister had lived her whole life alone and had never had a sexual partner. She hated anything that made her want to be sexual.

She didn't just hide her beauty and charm from other people; she also did things on purpose to make herself look ugly and unattractive.

Now that she had completely taken off the hijab and messed up her wavy, tan hair, she had a beautiful, angelic look that had nothing to do with how she used to look. It was like a beautiful butterfly came out of a rough cocoon and lit up the world with its beauty.

While I was lost in watching her, she suddenly moved and twisted her soft body. She then hit the grass a few times.

This sensual move got me more excited than anything else. But there were more surprises.

She lay face down on the grass, with her hips slightly higher than the rest of her body.

I'm not sure if she did it on purpose or because she had a lot of grass in her lower abdomen and lower body, which made her stand in such a lustful way.

No matter what the reason, it made me feel very sexy and broke all of my resistance.

After quickly and awkwardly taking off my clothes, I laid on top of her and kissed her from the back of her neck to her ankles.

We were both feeling a light, pleasant shake at the time.

No one thought we would be in such a situation. We felt like we had left our bodies on earth and were making love in the promised paradise.

After a while, we started to feel calmer and surer of ourselves.

For a brief moment, the big sister and I looked into each other's eyes.

I told her I was in love with her while I was caressing her lovely hair.

To tell the truth, these words were the result of lust overcoming my reason and logic, and they did not reflect my actual feelings for her.

In other words, I had lost control of my language and was expressing my love and interest in her in such a careless manner that you would think I was madly in love with her.

The big sister had a similar experience.

She spoke in a tone and manner reminiscent of drunk and delirious people.

"I want you." more than the entire world. "More than all the things I've ever worshiped!"

Then we hugged and kissed each other nonstop.

It is not an exaggeration to say that with each kiss we exchanged, we discovered and experienced something new deep within. It was as if we were walking through a new and unknown land, slowly revealing its secrets and wonders to us.

I'm not sure how long we stayed in this pleasant atmosphere. We had become so entwined that we had lost track of time. We didn't give a damn about it.

We were both at the peak of sexual pleasure at the time and didn't pay attention to what was going on around us.

When you reach this stage of sexual intercourse, you put aside feelings of shame and embarrassment and begin doing things you would consider less acceptable under normal circumstances.

I had a lot of fun flirting like this. At the same time, I was considering scaling a previously unclimbed peak.

To accomplish this goal, I had to move slowly and cautiously.

Otherwise, all of these introductions will be futile.

There was a chance that the big sister would be satisfied with this amount of sex and sexual interaction and would refuse to let me have more intimacy.

She had gotten what she wanted sexually and had her first taste of how sweet it was.

It did not, however, exhibit an inhibitory reaction. Her demeanor and movements suggested that she would like to accompany me until the end of this journey.

Now that I was certain, I prepared to conquer the forbidden land.

You have no idea how happy and proud I was to see the big sister in such a state.

She could no longer practice piety or avoid sin, and she saw this type of relationship as unhealthy and immoral. At least, she could not pretend in front of me anymore.

It was now time to strike the final blow before my lust faded and my penis fell from its ecstasy.

If such an incident occurred, I would be forever ashamed and embarrassed.

Her most valuable possession had been given to me by the big sister. As a result, I should not have passed up this opportunity at any cost.

Who would have thought that this woman, who seemed to be a saint, would lose her virginity to someone she and other people thought was an unbeliever and an atheist? What's more, I was doing it voluntarily and freely. That is, there was no use of force or violence.

It was a very important win for me. I still wasn't sure if she would let me do this, though.

When I was ready for penetration, she stepped back a little and asked,

"I heard it hurts a lot." "Is that right?"

I told her that this pain isn't that much and won't last long. But I couldn't make her feel better.

I was very set on doing this act, and I couldn't stop myself from doing it.

It was even possible to use force and get violent.

On the other side of the feed barn, I saw some glass containers. Then I had a sudden thought, so I asked the big sister,

"What's in those glasses?"

She turned her head to the other side while she was lying down and looked at those glasses.

Then she said,

"I think its olive oil,"

However, she didn't sound too sure.

One of my friends told me that I could use oil and other sticky things to make the pain go away.

At the same time, it makes people feel more sexually aroused and satisfied.

I oiled her thighs and the area around her genitalia very slowly and carefully.

It made her feel good and energized, and she asked me to oil her whole body because of it.

When I rubbed her nipples, I didn't even think about it, but her lust went to new heights.

She forced me to lie on the floor with my legs wide apart. Then she leaned over me from one side and started sucking my cock very hard. It felt like she was trying to squeeze all the life out of me.

Please forgive me for being so open with you about these problems. I just want you to look at this situation with a more open mind and not think about sexual relationships.

She did whatever she wanted with her lips and tongue, and it made me feel sexually excited and satisfied all over again.

In exchange, I did things that made her more aroused.

The last act of the show came on stage after this.

The big sister returned to her previous position and let me do the entire penetration and intercourse.

I did everything I could to finish this task in the best and most satisfying way possible.

Without exaggeration, I must say that I made it very well.

She didn't hurt or feel too bad, so she let me take out her hymen. You have no idea how satisfied it has made me. It felt like I had won a big battle. Of course, she bit me a few times while we were together.

I don't know if she did it because she was very sexually excited or because she felt pain and pressure during the penetration. At that time, the public didn't have much information about these issues, and most of what they knew about them came from guesses.

For example, people did not have any information about the reason for men's penises getting hard in the morning, which I experienced every few days. No one had yet said what the real reason was, though.

In any case, her bits not only didn't bother me or upset me, but they also made me feel more satisfied.

Then something happened that I've been afraid to talk about until now. But now that the pen has gone too far and lifted and torn the veils of modesty and purity, it is best to put everything straight and peeled on paper and let you be the judge.

The big sister told me to stand up straight and get up. Then she knelt in front of me and said,

"Pee on me!"

I already knew that some people act like this when they are sexually excited and aroused to the max. It might happen to people with a lot of power in society.

I read somewhere that these people get more sexual satisfaction by making themselves humiliated, which is not something everyone can understand or accept.

I happened to meet such people. But I never thought the big sister would ask me to do something like that.

It meant challenging her dying religious beliefs and convictions. Sleeping with one and having sex could be explained and dealt with in some way, but if this request she made on me was discovered, she would lose her entire reputation and social status.

Especially back then, when people didn't know much about these issues and didn't have much insight into them, even if no one finds out about this story and we keep it all to ourselves, it will still cause us trouble.

The least bad thing that could happen is that you would feel bad and embarrassed in front of the other person.

I didn't have any trouble with it at all. I was just afraid that the big sister would feel so bad after that about what she did that she would make me deal with the bad results.

She asked again, this time with a helpless look on her face as if she were praying to her god.

I said to myself,

"Why shouldn't I take this chance?" "I'm at the end of the line, so I might as well make the most of it."

With this as an excuse, I was ready to do what was thought to be the hardest thing I had ever done.

After a short pause, I put the tip of my finger on my penis, which was not erect and was bent, and turned to face him. Then I peed on her body, head, and face until there was nothing left.

So much did the big sister like it that I couldn't even imagine it; I thought I'd given her holy water.

At the same time, she was playing with her sexual organs and making sensual moans.

We were lucky because everyone was drunk and happy that night. If it wasn't that way, sh*t would have hit the fan.

There was only one problem left. The big sister had to immediately wash and clean herself.

Things were not going well for me. But we couldn't go to the bathroom at that time. There were a few barrels of clean water, which was enough for both of us to clean up.

We were cleaning ourselves while making jokes and laughing. A few times, we touched each other's lips and said nice things about each other.

Then, we all went out of the feed barn carefully, one by one, so as not to draw anyone's attention.

That night, I realized how close and unstable the line is between love and hate.

Indeed, our relationship was mostly based on lust and sexual need and not on love and spiritual connection. However, there were signs that things could get better in the future.

It happened to me, and it showed me that every moment of our lives brings challenges and big changes that can change our future.

Who would have thought that someone with an open mind like me would accept such a person? Before it happened, each of us called the other by the worst names and traits we could think of and saw it as a source of evil and destruction. But now we are trying to understand each other better and get to know each other better.

When I walked into my room, I saw my friends' shocked and interested faces. They had heard about our flirting.

They asked me to walk them through everything. It felt like I had just come back from a long trip full of strange and wonderful things.

I told them everything that went on between us as well.

As I had thought, they didn't take what I said too seriously and thought it was a joke.

They agreed that we had a relationship with each other, but they thought I was making things up about it. It didn't come as a surprise.

The big sister was so holy and obedient to what people thought were god's orders that this idea seemed impossible and far away.

They both smiled and said bravo when they were certain that what I said was correct.

At the same time, they told me that I needed to take better care of myself.

They told me that when the big sister's lust went away, she might reject me or even kill me. It is a secret that no one else should know.

However, I had already thought about all of these things and what could happen.

The only thing I could say was,

"You're right, my friends." "But I don't feel any regret, no matter what happens. Trust me, I'm telling you these words from the bottom of my heart."

Chapter Seven: Crossing

After this incident, a few weeks went by without anything bad happening to me. At the same time, the big sister behaved as if nothing special had happened between us.

However, this kind of behavior was completely normal and appropriate for the place and conditions we were living in.

As before, she was still deep in her spiritual and presumably holy body, telling others what to do and what not to do. I also read books and talked with my friends during the day.

At the same time, we tried to stay away from each other as much as possible and not face each other.

We wouldn't even look at other in the eyes. We were all embarrassed and ashamed of what had occurred. Especially the big sister, who believed she had done the worst thing possible.

I only got to talk to her once, at the Easter ceremony.

I did everything to make her feel sure that I would not tell anyone about our secret. Meanwhile, I engaged her in a brief philosophical dialogue, though not to probe the authenticity of her beliefs. All I wanted to do was ease her mind and make her feel a bit less guilty.

This situation went on for a while until we saw the first signs of spring and nature starting to grow again. Then, a bad and unpleasant thing happened during these days.

One morning, I heard that our old friend's health had gotten worse. As others told me, he got a very high fever and chills all of a sudden, and then he started showing signs and symptoms of a fatal and contagious disease. According to the big sister's decision and discretion, they had moved the old man downstairs.

As I said before, people who were very sick and close to dying were moved to this part of the building. No one was allowed in there under any circumstances, except during the patient's last hours of life.

Others were only allowed to go to this place at this time to say goodbye and take part in religious ceremonies.

I tried to visit the old man with the big sister's permission, but she angrily refused my request.

I wasn't too surprised by the way she treated me. If she was nice to me and behaved friendly and let me do something I wasn't typically allowed to do, the rumors that were going around behind our backs might get stronger.

We were cautious, but we could hear whispering coming from all directions, which worried us.

Anyhow, one of the nuns who didn't like the big sister helped us out and made it possible for us to visit our old friend.

Despite what they said and what we thought, our friend wasn't in a very bad situation. The color of his face and the way he looked indicated that he was in poor health, but he wasn't so sick that we gave up all hope of him getting better.

In this situation, the only thing we could do was take away his complete hopelessness and despair and give him encouragement and strength.

Unfortunately, it was a useless effort and we didn't achieve anything at all. I thought he didn't have a lot of time left. If things weren't this way, he wouldn't have told us his last wish.

He wanted to get away from this painful place in any way he could and live his last days with complete and unconditional freedom. In fact, it was what we all wished for.

Undoubtedly, we were able to grant him his last wish and ensured him that he would not leave this world feeling sad. But we needed to move quickly and think things through.

If his condition was getting worse than this, we could not make his wish come true, which was a real pity.

***

A few days after this happened, we got lucky unexpectedly, which gave us a good chance to break out of the monastery.

The big sister, along with several nuns and her servants, went to the lower village to watch the examination and trial of a person who had helped the intruders get into the monastery while they were doing religious ceremonies.

People said he was a local wanderer who used a lie to get into the monastery the day before this incident and hid in a place where no one could see him.

I don't know how they caught this person or how they did it, but I was sure that he would not get a fair trial.

Anyway, we took advantage of this chance and quietly left the monastery. We were, of course, all prepared for this moment.

We would be in trouble if we went down this path without enough food and water and warm, good clothes.

We couldn't go through the mountains yet because the weather wasn't good enough. But the biggest problem was that we were traveling with someone who was very sick and had a lot of trouble moving around.

He had trouble moving easily, let alone he could walk with us. Only putting him on a horse or mule would work. But unfortunately, neither horses nor mules were left in the stable.

So there was only one thing we could do. We each had to carry him piggyback in turn. It is clear how hard and time-consuming it was, especially for me, who didn't have much strength.

It was almost around midday when we got close to the crossing, exhausted and worn out. The monastery was easily visible from there, standing out like a black and ugly stain in nature's lap.

We stayed there for a little while to catch our breath, and then we kept going.

If we kept going this way, it was likely that we would reach the low slopes of the mountain before sunset, and by then, the big sister and her followers wouldn't be able to get to us.

Mother Nature didn't agree with us, though, and all of a sudden there was a strong wind and a storm. We also had to stop moving and take cover under a big rock that looked like it had a cave in it.

Our sick friend was in a very bad state at the time. He coughed all the time and shook like a leaf.

If we hadn't started a fire and made him hot food right away, he would have lost all his strength and energy and wouldn't have been able to keep going.

We were all aware that starting a fire in such conditions was not a good idea. Certainly, the big sister must have heard by then that we had gotten away.

We were sure that the first thing she would do was to send experienced and professional people after us to keep track and find us. Without a doubt, every footprint and trace we left would make it harder for us to get out of that terrible hell.

But to save the life of our friend we had to take this risk.

I accepted to collect firewood, which was not an easy job at all. Nearby, there was almost no dry grass or brush. The heavy rain over the past few days was the reason why. It took us about an hour before we could finally start a fire and make a quick meal. We made coffee to wake us up and keep us warm.

The poor old man had gotten so weak that he could not chew and digest his food well. We had to chop up the food and give it to him slowly over a cup of coffee.

We also set up a place for him where he could rest and get some energy back. But it didn't look like he could go with us on this hard and dangerous path.

While I was setting up his bed, he grabbed my hand and said to both of us in a way that sounded like he was about to leave us and say goodbye:

"I appreciate everything. You two have been my best friends for me. I wish I could repay some of your kindness and affection if I lived long enough."

"Oh my friend, don't talk like this. We still have a lot of adventures and fun to look forwards to. You thought we'd leave you alone so easily."

He forced a smile and said,

"Friend, it (death) is something that we cannot do anything about. Anyway, I'm very glad to take my last breath outside and I owe you this."

We did all our best to give him strength, hope, and reasons to keep going, but it was no longer useful.

He was prepared to confront death and didn't appear to be terrified of it.

In this situation, the only thing we could do was stay up all night with him and take turns nursing him. We hoped that a miracle would happen and things would get better.

We were both very tired and needed to rest and get new energy. But we took good care of our friend who was sick and dying.

When it was almost dawn, we realized that his soul had left his body and he was no longer in pain or suffering. At least he was glad that he had been able to spend the last moments of his life in a free space where he wished.

We buried his body quickly nearby. It was a place where the enemies could not find it and also somewhere that we could find it easily later.

We buried him respectfully and decently, in a way that matched the honor and status of this noble and free man.

Then we got our luggage and ran as fast as we could to the crossing. However, the wind was very strong, the weather got worse and stormier the farther we went.

Even a few steps ahead of us were hard to see.

It was hard and a little crazy to cross the crossing in those conditions.

But we had made up our minds and didn't worry about the dangers that lay ahead. In other words, we were both willing to face the wind, the storm, and the sharp and fragile rocks until we went back the way we came and put ourselves in the hands of the ignorance that lives deep in the mountains.

At the same time, we thought back to the words and rumors that said something like a monster lived deep in the mountains. We didn't believe in any of these things because we thought they were based on ignorance and superstition. However, due to the nature of the situation, our thoughts picked up on these details without our knowledge.

As we went further, the road got much narrower and harder to pass on. It got to the point where two people couldn't easily walk next to each other.

At any time, one of us could have slipped and fallen into the bottom of a terrible valley that had just opened up under our feet.

We moved very slowly and carefully so that something like this wouldn't happen. It took us almost a whole day to cross the pass safely and get to the low, flat mountain slopes. But we were so tired and weak that we couldn't go any further.

We should have found a safe place to rest, eat, and get our breath back. If that didn't happen, we'd both faint.

We smoked a cigarette and talked for a time after we ate and drank coffee. We were both delighted and proud at the moment, and we were pretty convinced we had gotten rid of the big sister and her bigoted followers. But we quickly realized we had made a big mistake.

We were still fatigued when the dark silhouettes of numerous persons came into view from afar.

They were looking for us for sure. It was clear from the way they moved that they had been following us. So there was no time to waste.

We quickly got our humble belongings and ran as fast as we could down the mountain. This quick and sudden move caught their attention and made the situation more dangerous for us.

They pulled the horses towards us and galloped very fast. At the same time, they kept firing at us. Even though they were almost too far away from us, I have to say that they shot very well and accurately.

One of the bullets hit a stone slab in front of me right next to my head. I was lucky that I didn't kick the bucket in that situation.

They were quite clear about what they wanted to express. They had no choice but to bring us back to the monastery, alive or dead, and hand us over to their lord.

In the situations like this, the big sister never joked with anyone and never made an exception.

She probably wouldn't mind if I went away and she never had to think about that night again. It was the only way for her to be sure that I would keep quiet and not tell anything to anybody.

At the same time, as I was running down the slope of the mountain, I thought about the big sister and imagined her in my mind.

She was standing over my grave and staring at my dead body with that cold look and contemptuous smile.

I didn't want to get there at any cost.

We could only be saved if we got to the bottom of the mountain quickly and crossed the river. It was the last thing that kept us from being free. But it turned out to be much harder than we thought.

At that time of year, the river was very full, and crossing it took a lot of bravery. We have already given this some thought. We had a good plan for how to get past this barrier. But the only problem we faced in that situation was the lack of enough time to carry out our plan. So there was only one thing we could do.

We had to jump into the cold, fast-moving water and find a way to get across the river in any way possible. If not, we would end up in the hands of people who didn't care much about keeping us alive. At least I should be thankful that I was with a person who was experienced enough.

Sergeant Smith had worked on a boat before the war and he was familiar with situations like this.

He went into the river before me to measure how deep and fast the water was moving. Even though it wasn't needed! Whether it was good or bad, we had to cross that raging river.

He was able to quickly and easily get to the middle of the river. It was like he was going through a small and undisturbed stream.

Then he pointed at me and told me to follow him carefully. I likewise plunged into the water and followed the same course, but it was more difficult for me.

I could see that the water flow on the other side of the river was much stronger as I came closer to him.

It is most common if the river descends more sharply. In any case, we had no choice but to confront this enormous, inexorable force.

I trusted my trip companion so fully that I closed my eyes and just followed him.

He swam rapidly and expertly, and he showed no symptoms of fatigue or weakness.

If we kept going like this, we would probably get away from those who are after us. In this case, we would be the first people who got rid of the big sister and her followers safely.

Obviously, it was possible as long as they didn't leave their territory and didn't follow us across the river. I was visualizing the sweet dream of freedom when Mother Nature showed her harsh and cruel side more openly. My dear friend couldn't keep his balance until the very end. He finally gave in to the strong current of water, which carried him down the river like a cotton doll.

I was stunned for a few seconds and didn't do anything. In other words, I wasn't able to do anything special.

If I tried to swim towards it, the fast current of the water would take me with it too.

At the time, the only thing I could do was follow him down the river and figure out how to get him out of the water before he got frostbite and gave up attempting to save his life.

It took me a while to get out of the water and do something to help him. At that time, I didn't care about my situation or who was after us. All I cared about was saving my friend, who was getting farther away from me by the second.

I managed to reach him quickly. I got the opportunity to take him out of the water once or twice while he was struggling. But right at the end, he ran out of energy, making my efforts useless.

But I didn't stop trying over and over again to save his life.

It happened when I was weak.

I was to give up and surrender to the hard and breathtaking circumstances. However, there remained a glimmer of hope.

In its lower parts, the river got narrower and stopped roaring as loudly as it had at first.

So there was still a chance I could pull him out of the water.

I sped up my steps and kept running along the river, even though I was very tired and weak. Fortunately, I got there before him.

I looked for something I could use to pull him out of the water right away.

It was a pity that I had left my rope by the river, if not, I could have helped him more easily and better. In the end, I chose a branch that was pretty big and strong. I made a plan to get as close to him as I could and give him the branch of a tree so that he could grasp it and pull himself out of the water.

I jumped on a rock in the middle of the river and stretched out to him with the branch when he reached the narrowest point of the river. He could do it as well. But he was too weak to hang on for long, so he let it go before I could bring him toward myself.

I couldn't do anything else, and after that everything was up to her luck.

Both of us were prepared for the worst that might happen to us.

But we didn't think we'd be separated so painfully.

While I was desperately trying to follow him with my eyes, someone came up behind me and hit me so hard with a hard object that the world went dark before my eyes.

***

When I woke up, I found myself in a cart with my hands tied. The cart was going over a very rough and uneven road.

When I tried to move my body someone kicked me hard in the side and said,

"Stay still and don't move, if you don't, I will shoot you."

Then, he murmured some bad words to me. From their point of view, I was just an atheist, and it was also permissible for them to kill me. So I should have kept careful and not given them a reason to do what they did.

As soon as we got to the monastery, they took me to my room and locked the door. At least I was glad I wasn't sent to that awful crypt and was not prosecuted.

One of the nuns who liked me a lot, came into my room a few times and took care of me. At the same time, she told me what was going on in the world outside. As she said the story of our escape had made the people of the monastery very passionate and excited. Some of them had even thought about coming after us. This situation in the monastery made me happy on the one hand, but it also worried me on the other.

If the big sister and the people who are close to her heard these words and rumors, they would probably act violently towards me to teach others a lesson.

When I woke up the next morning, the colonel was standing next to my bed, looking at me with an angry face.

I was not sure if he came here because of what my friends and I had done or if he just happened to be there. It was also possible that he had arrived to deal with the situation of that fugitive soldier.

Either way, his sudden and unexpected arrival increased my anxiety and made my future more uncertain.

Even though I was upset and angry with him, as soon as I saw him, I gave him a military salute and showed my respects in the same state.

The colonel also responded to me.

Then he sat down next to me and said in a scolding voice,

"What a dumb thing you did. I did not expect something like this from you. You embarrassed me and made me feel bad in front of the big sister."

I answered him,

"If you were in my place and lived here for a while, you would probably choose the same path I took."

"What did not you have here that you put yourself into trouble because of that? Were your conditions here worse than the war conditions?"

"So you don't know what's going on here?!

The colonel continued more gently,

"I agree that there are a lot of rules and limits here. This is something that everyone agrees on. But you did not come here to have fun. Did you?"

"That's right. But there are things here that..."

"I don't want to hear any more about it. You should go and apologize to the big sister right now. If you don't, you will be severely punished. I can no longer do anything."

- I'm sorry very much, sir. I cannot fulfill your request.

"So I have to move you to the front line. You know where I mean"

"No problem, sir. In wartime, a person could die at any time, but it is better than letting his pride and dignity be trampled from morning to night.

"Were you supposed to spend the rest of your life here? You could have waited for a little while if you wanted to feel better."

"The problem is not just me. Some things are happening here that no one can remain indifferent to. At least I can't stand it."

The colonel said with more anger and fury,

"It's all my fault. I shouldn't have sent someone like you here. I knew you would end up making trouble.

"What did I do except that I did not accept their bullying?"

"You stood against these people's religion and beliefs. This is not something small."

"So you agree with them. I did not expect it at all."

"I'm too busy right now to argue with you. The big sister told me to handle this situation."

"So I should be grateful! If I didn't, I would die the same way as the others. What are you going to do with me?"

The colonel walked around the room and started wrangling with himself.

Then, when he answered me,

"I'm sorry to say this, but you need to get ready for a military trial."

I asked him stunningly,

"For what crime?"

To explain his decision, he said,

"You killed three people with what you did. There were two people with you and one of the people who were looking for you fell off the edge of the cliff and died."

In my defense, I said,

"The people who came with me chose it themselves. But I don't think I did anything wrong. The people who made us do it have to be blamed."

Anyway, I can't overlook your guilt easily. I mean, the law doesn't allow me to do that, but I promise you'll have a chance to defend yourself.

"But sir here is not the army. Only a few dogmatic nuns run here. So you don't have to be so strict."

"I wish it were as easy as what you say. Unfortunately, several delicate concerns, in this case, are difficult to overlook. After all, when you came here you were serving the army. So, you will be treated according to applicable military law."

"You must be kidding me. Don't you have a relationship with the big sister that you take her side that much?"

"I turned a deaf ear to what you said. I would think of a strong defense for myself right now if I were you. Believe me, they are very serious charges."

I didn't believe that the colonel had said these lies and nonsense.

He couldn't convict me with such a weak and incorrect argument unless he utilized his authority and influence.

I was naive to believe that because he had known my family for a long time, he could assist me to get out of this mess.

We used to be good friends who never said no when each other needed help or did each other a favor. But at that time we were on two opposite fronts.

In the next few conversations, we talked about things that took away my last hope and made it clear what my duty was.

I got a thousand distinct frightening notions and thoughts all at once when he left me alone.

Believe me, I wasn't concerned about a military trial or what might happen later. I just didn't want to get into trouble with this stupidity, especially at a time when our country was poised to undergo a major political and social transformation.

When one of the nuns brought me some food and water, I was thinking and dreaming about the same things.

She behaved as if she was feeding the last meal of a person who is sentenced to death.

I tried to get her to say something and find out more about what had happened. But it didn't help.

The poor girl was so frightened and worried that she couldn't even say a word.

This crazy and scary situation went on all day and into the night. In the meantime, one or two crew members came to see me and asked how I was doing. But there was no sign of the big sister.

When I woke up, it was almost midnight and I could hear several people laughing loudly. It looked like the monastery was having a party!

When I listened up carefully, I found that the noise was coming from downstairs where those unlucky nuns used to live.

No one went to that room since they were dead and buried. One of the nuns told others and swore that she had seen some ghosts there as they were dancing and singing happily. The ghosts' story made the people of the monastery very terrified and horrified to the point that no one would dare to go there unless they were compelled to.

Let's skip this point, the noises kept going on for so long that I finally got up and looked down through the hole in the room's floor. When I looked up, I saw the colonel drinking and having fun with two young nuns. Then, I knew why he support the big sister and took her side so much.

In reality, he was a wolf in sheep's clothing. He was a very mean and dishonest person he didn't deserve to wear the military uniform.

I don't know how we've been friends for so long and I didn't realize this point about him. Now that I knew what he looked like, I felt less safe and more worried. But at that time, I was more concerned about those innocent girls.

It was clear from their expressions and movements that they were disgusted and forced to have sexual intercourse with these demons.

It didn't seem likely that the big sister would give them such permission.

I agreed that she lately violated some of her moral rules and values and did some weird and unexpected things, but I found it difficult to believe that she had been aware of what was happening here.

Most likely, they did so where she couldn't see. There were, of course, other ideas. She might have been aware of what was happening here, but she didn't do anything about it for some unknown reasons. Anyway, witnessing such a scene made me extremely shocked and the desire to take revenge on them suddenly flared up in me.

As they were drunk, they talked and did disgusting things which would make any intelligent and aware person ashamed and humiliated.

On the one hand, these heinous deeds demonstrated how awful they were, while on the other, and the other, it was a clear betrayal of the principles and values for which thousands of people had died.

If our adversaries found out about this happening, they would create so much noise and talk so negatively about us with no end.

By then, I knew very well what might happen to me too. If I hadn't thought about my condition as soon as I could, I would have been found guilty and sentenced harshly. It was also possible that I would receive a death sentence and get hanged.

As I was immersing in these thoughts, the door opened, and the big sister along with the hunchbacked man came in.

I thought for a moment that I was done.

The big sister was quite upset and confused and she often was wrangling with herself. It seemed like she was trying to do or say something she couldn't.

She was like this for a short time. Then she knelt in front of me and with a tone full of despair and shame said,

"I made a lot of mistakes that harmed many people who did not deserve it. But now I need to change and improve myself. I just wanted to beg for your help.

I was stunned and couldn't believe it, so I said,

"How may I help you?"

The big sister looked and pointed downstairs and added,

"Those girls are victims. They are victims of people like me, who have lived incorrectly their entire lives, and have harmed them with their ignorance and brutality. So help me save them and get rid of these demons. "

"So, did you know that this room's floor has a crack?"

"A few days ago, I saw it. So, I brought you here so you could see everything with our own eyes. Now, tell me if you're going to help me or not."

I replied with no hesitation,

"You can count on my help, sister. But first, please answer my question. Why haven't you said anything up until now?"

"Because I didn't know anything about it."

"How can something like this happen right next to you and you not notice it?"

"Believe me, I was totally in the dark and I have no idea what was happening here. If I were aware of everything, I would have taught them a good lesson."

"Why haven't the girls talked about it before? You won't find this strange."

"They probably did it to save their faces. Maybe the colonel said something bad to them. It can't be anything other than these two possibilities."

"How did you figure it out?"

But this isn't relevant right now. We won't get anywhere unless we do this.

"I got it by accident. But this is not the point right now. We must first retaliate in whatever way possible before they leave this place. If we don't do that, we cannot do anything about it later."

Have you thought about what to do?

The big sister took a colt out from under her priestly robe and said,

"It shouldn't be too hard. Just give them a little time to get completely drunk. Then we will be done with our plan."

"What were you trying to say? You might not want to kill them!"

"No, I only armed myself for safety. We have no idea what will happen."

"Could you tell me where you got this gun?"

"Behind the feed store, one of the crew members found it. I think it belonged to those men who attacked the monastery a few months ago."

"Now, pick up this gun and come with us. Don't be too worried. I'm sure we'll have no trouble with any of them."

The big sister talked as if she was going to do something simple and common.

I thought that she was going to kill them. She had killed and broken the law for some things smaller than these. Although her hands were not stained with blood, because of her ideas and thoughts, she became the cause of many terrible and cruel things that gave goosebumps to everyone.

Although the colonel and his companions deserved harsh punishments for sure that would teach them a lesson, I didn't want to kill them.

During the war, it was seen as a clear and terrible act of treachery and no motivations and objectives could be used to justify why a person did it.

After some talk, it was decided to catch them off guard while they were doing their dirty actions and take their weapons. Then, we would take them to the monastery crypt, lock them up, and wait for the authorities to come and tell us what to do with them. I did not doubt that this plan wouldn't work, but it would be better than making our hands dirty to their blood.

I simply hoped that everything went according to their plan and wishes, since if not, we'd have to resort to force and violence.

They seemed eager and determined, but I didn't think it would be easy for them.

It was not easy, especially for the big sister, who didn't know much about these things and whose only talent was to pick on sick people and poor, innocent nuns. If it had been a shootout and a pitched battle, we would have been the losers on this field for sure.

We were up against people who knew about military art and techniques and didn't give up so easily. As a result, any mistake or slip could cost us our lives and put the other people living in the monastery in danger.

When I told her about this problem, she did something interesting and unexpected.

First, she took off her religious robe. Then she took a step forwards and said with a determined and strong voice,

"Now we'll see who isn't ready."

I never thought I'd see the big sister in a situation like this and with such outfits one day. She looked like a brave, rebellious woman who stood up for something other than her ideals and religious values.

***

We waited for a half hour until the colonel and his friends got drunk and couldn't think straight. Only because of their inebriation were we able to catch them off guard and quickly defeated them.

They didn't believe a covert alliance and arrangement could be formed against them. They wouldn't have been so cold and uncaring if they had. They didn't even close the door completely.

When I looked through the crack in the door, I saw something I couldn't have dreamed up even in my worst nightmares.

They tied the girls' hands and feet from behind, then threw them onto the bed.

They poured alcohol on them while whipping their backs and hips at the same time.

This disgusting and crazy behavior stimulated them more and gave their sick souls more pleasure.

When the big sister observed what was going on, she became so furious and enraged that she forgot our plans and everything we had said and attacked them like a lunatic.

The colonel and his friends were naked and had nothing to defend themselves with. They had drunk so much that it was hard for them to even stand up, let alone fight back.

It was the first time I'd ever seen my commander so weak and helpless.

While I was still stunned, the big sister grabbed a large butcher's knife from behind her clothes! Then she dashed towards the colonel as fast as she could, and before I could stop her, she smacked him on the back. The colonel made such a loud lament that I got goosebumps. He immediately slid to the ground and curled up like a snake.

The other two men were too scared to do anything special.

The big sister slapped them both hard and said bad words to them. It was as if she was punishing two naughty and playful kids.

After that, she put her paw in the colonel's long hair and lifted his head just a little so they could look each other in the eyes. She looked into the depth of his sad, dying eyes for a few moments without saying anything.

It was clear that she enjoyed treating him like this. It seemed like she was having a religious ceremony.

Then, in a voice full of anger and hate, she said,

"You used your power and position to satisfy your dirty desires. Now it's time to pay back what you've earned."

The sister was so mad and upset that she would have done anything.

I moved closer and whispered in her ear,

"We don't need to be so violent. They can no longer do anything."

The big sister looked at me with anger and said,

"Right now, I have to execute the divine decree on them." If that doesn't happen, they would get away with their punishment."

I tried to take the knife from her, but she got mad and pushed me away. When a person gets so angry, she sees red and she doesn't use her reason or logic. Instead, she decides what to do based on her emotions.

The big sister asked her slavish servant to hold me tightly and not let me move.

Then, right in front of my shocked eyes, he cut the colonel's throat and pulled his last breaths off.

When the colonel's friends saw this terrible scene, they started to cry and beg for their lives. At that moment, they showed no sign of manly pride or strength, and they had reached the lowest point of shame.

The big sister told me to hurry up and kill them.

I already had enough problems and troubles, and I didn't want to add to them.

Yes, I agree that the colonel and his companions' death would have been better for me, but, as a soldier and a patriot, I couldn't bring myself to do anything so heinous.

They had no weapons and couldn't defend themselves.

Therefore, there was no good reason or excuse for killing them. Instead, it sounds like it was done to take revenge.

I told the big sister very clearly and openly what I thought and asked her not to do that. But she did not want to listen to me at all.

She wanted those two people to die and refused to listen to any explanation or argument to the contrary.

We were debating about it when I heard the dreadful sound of two gunshots flying from behind and trembled my eardrums. The two people then collapsed and died difficulty.

You may already know what happened. The man with the hunchback listened to what the big sister asked and killed those two officers.

I had no idea he had a weapon as well. If I did, I would have been more careful.

Anyway, it was finished, and we'd all have to deal with the consequences sooner or later unless we come up with a good idea and plan for it.

We had to get rid of the dead bodies as soon as possible, which was the first thing we had to do. At the same time, we needed to come up with a plausible explanation for why the colonel and his assistants were lost.

There was no doubt about it that we gave wicked individuals what they deserved for what they did. However, we had no clear evidence of this assertion other than our own words and the confessions of nuns who would claim to have been sexually harassed.

Compared to the false pride of the colonel, our words didn't have much weight, and they wouldn't have been accepted so easily. In that situation, the only thing we could do was deny the truth and get rid of all the evidence.

We stayed up all night and started to get rid of what was left.

We started by getting rid of the dead bodies. We buried them somewhere no person could reach them. Then, we cleaned all the signs of that bloody fight and it was as if nothing had occurred.

When morning came, we were so tired that we didn't have the strength to get up. But there was one more thing that needed to be accomplished.

The big sister told everyone who worked at the monastery and lived there to meet inside the compound. Everyone pretty much knew what had happened the night before and none of them believed that what had happened was our fault.

Everybody was happy and thankful for what had happened the night before. But the big sister gave them the advice they needed so they wouldn't say something that would cause trouble for everyone.

She then advised them to think about the conditions which were ahead of us and consider what was going on and make the right decision about their future.

It was the first time that she considered how others thought and believed and she was doing something contrary to her religious and moral values.

One of them asked,

"Does that mean we can leave right now?"

The big sister smiled reassuringly and said,

"Of course, my daughter. Be sure nobody here can stop you."

As was expected, most of the young nuns didn't want to stay there.

They took off their religious veils right in front of us and ran away. They were like young birds that take their first flight.

Now, the big sister, some of her followers, and I were left in the monastery. Also, the man with the hunched back who seemed to have nowhere else to go stayed with us.

The big sister made a motion and told them to leave us alone for a minute.

They already knew that we had some special relationships. It was clear from the way they looked at each other and smiled. But it didn't matter much to us in that situation.

The big sister came up to me and asked very sincerely,

"What do you want to do now?"

I also told her the truth and answered her frankly,

"I want to go home. I don't know for sure if I still have a house, but I'll try my luck."

"So you don't want to go back to the front lines of the war?"

"It wouldn't be a good idea for me to appear in the war under these conditions. Besides, I'm still not well enough to take up arms and fight for what I believe in."

"But you were very brave last night. I was very lucky to have a man like you by my side in this situation. If you weren't there, we don't know what would have happened to us."

I was somehow embarrassed and answered,

"It is your kindness, sister, I just did my human duty."

"You're too modest. No one else can do what you did. You should be proud of yourself."

"You were incredibly courageous and reckless last night too. I'm delighted I wasn't standing in front of you."

"Please don't hold that against me. I know I went too far. But I don't have any regrets about it. Those buggers did something that made my blood boil."

"Sister, I'd like to know something. Why did you send so many people to look for us? Sergeant Smith would still be alive if you hadn't done that. This incident might not have happened either."

"At that time I had to do something, not because I wanted to. It was mainly for the sake of others that I did such a stupid thing. But now I don't care where I stand. Believe me, I say it from the bottom of my heart."

"Sister, let's not talk about it anymore. I'd rather ask you a personal question about that night."

"Why not? There is no longer a curtain between us. So ask anything you like. Rest assured that I will tell you the truth when I answer."

"I'm still in awe of how quickly you changed. What actually happened to change you so drastically?"

"Despite what you might think, it did not happen all at once. You once said that we can't run away from our natural needs. Believe me, I never went a day without thinking about sexual matters. I even made a copy of the Kamasutra book in secret.

"Are you serious?"

I could show you. But some of the unexpected and surprising things I did that night, were a kind of punishment for me.

"You mean you did not do them out of desire?"

"No, I'm not saying I didn't like it. But I wanted to humiliate myself in some way. Do you get what I'm saying?"

"Yes, sister. You shouldn't be worried about it."

"I have to say that the sexual relationship I had that night was the best I've ever had. I thank you for that."

At this moment, the big sister looked around and then moved a little closer to me.

She wanted to give me one last embrace and kiss. But it was still very difficult for her to openly express what was truly on her mind.

I didn't know what to do as I looked at her because she looked different and more beautiful without her hijab. I saw that she had put on some makeup when I looked at her carefully. Her lips looked pinker and fresher than ever.

Her dark brown hair was groomed well, giving it a form that complemented her face.

Now let's talk about her captivating smile, cuteness, and charisma, which all made my heart race and kept me more intrigued than ever.

She drew me into her arms and gave me the longest, sweetest kiss of my life as soon as we were both alone.

When I left my sick body in her warm, miraculous arms, I thought to take her with me to the land of my ancestors and start a new life away from all these problems and prejudices. Yes, you did hear correctly. I was falling in love with someone who had been my worst enemy and who I hated very much.

When I talked about my decision with her, she was as happy as a newly-married woman. But very quickly, signs of worry and doubt showed up on her face.

She turned away from me slowly and went back to the monastery. It was as if she couldn't leave that place so easily. I went after her and asked,

"Why don't you just leave here?" You still care about this place, right?

The big sister smiled bitterly and sadly and said,

"I wish I could, my love. But I have to stay here and pay for what I have done."

"You shouldn't blame yourself for things that have already happened."

"You did these things because you were prejudiced and lacked knowledge. What matters is that you have changed and want to begin a new life."

The sister turned to me and said in a sad voice,

"I have to stay here and fix some things". If not, someone else like me will be found and ruin many people's lives."

"Does that mean we can no longer see each other?"

"I don't know how to answer your question. We might see each other soon if we're lucky and time goes the way we want it to. But if it did not take place, I would pray for you forever."

"Now, please get out of this hellhole and save yourself. Do not look behind you."

The big sister said these last words as she found her throat obstructed and she was to sobbing. When she went back to the monastery and shut the door on me, I could hear her crying, which made me sad and happy at the same time. I was happy because I could see how much she had changed and become purer.

But in reality, her painful cry was because of her lost life and the opportunities she missed when she was stuck on empty principles and values.

It happened many years ago and after that, I couldn't see her anymore.

However, I wrote her a few letters and asked how she was doing, but she never answered my letters.

Anyway, the memories of that time, both good and bad, stayed with me, and they helped me realize that people can grow and change no matter under what conditions.

All they have to do is look again at how deeply they believe and not be afraid of doubts.